HOT FOR YOU

Formatting and Interior Design by Bella Media Management.

First Pink Zebra Publishing Paperback Edition

ISBN-13: 978-1492867265

HOT FOR YOU

Cheyenne McCray

Pink zebra publishing
Scottsdale, Arizona

CHAPTER 1

Leigh's phone must be off. Carilyn pressed her own iPhone's disconnect button and tucked it back into her purse. Leigh had said she'd be home all day but Carilyn's calls kept going straight to voicemail. But then again, Carilyn was two hours early.

She steered her car down a busy street and glanced at a place named the Hummingbird Café, which was next door to a bar called Nectars. Her stomach growled, making her decision for her. While she waited for Leigh to call her back, she had to get something to put in her belly. The café looked like a great place to get lunch.

She drove around until she found a place to park, behind the building. It must be a great place if she had to park around the back. After she killed the engine, she grabbed her purse and climbed out. She tugged down her thigh-length jean skirt, shut the door, and locked her car.

It had been a long drive from Kansas City to Prescott, even with the stops she'd made and the overnight stay at a hotel in Albuquerque. She pushed fiery red curls that had escaped from her ponytail away from her face and headed around the building toward the front entrance. It was a beautiful Arizona spring day and she smiled to herself. Back home in Kansas it was still chilly but here the weather was gorgeous. Arizona was so different than the Midwest.

Through the plate glass window, she saw that the café was busy and she hoped there was an available table. It was a quaint-looking place with a blue and white striped awning, flower boxes filled with geraniums on the windowsills, and a large hummingbird and flowers painted on the front window. Ironwork tables with matching chairs were arranged on the patio in front of the restaurant. Each table was occupied and the sound of conversation filled the air.

Bells jangled on the door as she pushed it open and immediately warm delicious smells met her nose. Her stomach growled again.

A woman with short blonde hair stood at the hostess stand and smiled at Carilyn. "Welcome to the Hummingbird. Will anyone be joining you?"

Carilyn shook her head. "Just me."

The hostess showed Carilyn to a table near the window. She sat in the chair and glanced out the window at the busy street before taking a look at the menu.

After a pretty waitress had taken Carilyn's order for a club sandwich with home fries, Carilyn drew her phone out of her purse and pulled up a map for directions to Leigh's house. Her friend didn't live too far away, but Carilyn never dropped in on anyone unless she knew they were home and they were expecting her. Leigh wasn't expecting Carilyn for quite a while yet.

Her gaze drifted away from the map and back to the window. Her eyes rested on the backside of a man standing in front of the café, who was holding a phone to his ear. He had a powerful build and his navy blue T-shirt stretched across his broad shoulders. He wore pants that hugged his nice ass and his athletic thighs. The shirt had Prescott Fire Department across the back. She wondered if he looked as yummy from the front as he did from the back and she hoped he would turn around.

Still on his phone, he faced the restaurant, granting her wish. She sighed as her gaze traveled over his muscular chest and up to his handsome face and his chestnut brown hair. If all firefighters looked as good as he did, she might have to set fire to the kitchen while she was here.

She cocked her head as she remembered that Leigh was dating a fireman. Was this the guy? If he was, Leigh was one lucky woman.

The firefighter shoved his phone into a holster on his belt and walked to the café's entrance. The bells jangled as he entered and he greeted the hostess with a grin that made Carilyn sigh again. She wouldn't mind having that sexy grin directed her way, up close and personal.

Mentally, she shook her head. She was only going to be in Prescott for a month, so no sense in drooling over hot firefighters here. Not to mention she'd promised herself she wasn't going to rush into another relationship after Sam went into the Peace Corps six months ago. He'd broken her heart but she still cared for him and hoped he was doing well.

She didn't even know why she was thinking about relationships when she was eleven hundred miles away from home.

Rather than looking away from the man, she continued to watch him—it was as if her gaze was glued to him. After the hostess led him to a table not too far from Carilyn, the hostess left him with one menu. Apparently he was eating alone, too.

The man raised his head. Eyes the color of polished oak met hers and the corner of his mouth turned up as he smiled. Her face warmed and she was afraid she was turning red—a curse of being so fair-skinned. She looked away from him and back to her phone. Of course the screen had gone dark so she quickly pressed a button to bring the map back up. The screen blurred as she felt the heat of his gaze on her.

Thankfully, the waitress arrived with Carilyn's club sandwich. She would just focus on her lunch and not look at the firefighter again. Yet, she couldn't help herself and snuck one more look at him from beneath her lashes. That was one damn fine man.

The sandwich was great as were the home fries, satisfying her hunger. Doing her best not to look at the man again, she paid her bill and left the restaurant. She didn't know if she'd imagined it, but she felt warmth on her skin, like he was watching her leave.

A breath of relief rushed out of her once she made it outside. Now she could stop drooling over hot firefighters and get back to real life.

Leigh still hadn't returned Carilyn's call, so she tried her friend again as she walked down the sidewalk. The day was sunny and warm and a few people walked along the street in unhurried strides. Everyone looked so casual and relaxed.

She listened to the phone ring. Once more the call went directly to voicemail. She'd left a couple of messages earlier, so she pressed the off button, breaking the connection.

An acrid odor came from ahead and she frowned. It smelled like something was burning.

When she rounded the building she froze. Smoke billowed from a car—

Her car.

Panicked, she raised her phone to dial 9-1-1, but her fingers were trembling and it slipped out of her hand. Just as she stooped to pick it up, someone rushed past her.

She heard the squawk of a radio and saw that the firefighter from the café was running toward a truck, radio held up to his mouth with one hand, keys gripped in his opposite fist. He shoved the radio into a holster and jerked opened the truck door. He grabbed something red and she saw that it was a fire extinguisher.

"Get back." He shouted over his shoulder and she almost tripped over her own feet as she hurried to back up.

Fire crackled and hissed and her heart pounded. Even from where she stood, she felt the heat of the flames now coming from the car's interior.

The firefighter had already started using the extinguisher, but the flames were growing too rapidly. Sirens filled the air and a part of her realized the fire department must have been close because in the next moment a fire truck pulled up behind the café. Immediately the fireman from the café tossed aside the spent extinguisher, hurried to the truck, and started working with his fellow firefighters.

Everything was a blur to Carilyn as the men hooked up a hose to a nearby fire hydrant and in the next moment the firefighters aimed a powerful burst of water on the car.

Then it hit her hard and she gripped her hands into fists. Her laptop was on the floorboard of the backseat of her car. It was more important than everything in the car combined and it was most definitely history. All she could do was watch as her car burned along with her livelihood.

Helplessly, she stared at the scene, her heart already having sunk to her toes. The fire was out within minutes, but her car was toast, along with everything in it.

Two police cruisers arrived and officers blocked off the area, keeping the growing crowd back, away from the scene.

The firefighter from the café turned and looked at her. He was the only one not wearing protective fire fighting gear and smoke streaked his face and bare arms. He started walking toward her.

"Your car?" he asked when he reached her.

Unable to speak, she nodded.

He dragged his hand down his face. "Are you all right, Miss—?"

"Thompson." She swallowed as she found her voice. "I'm Carilyn Thompson."

"I'm Cody McBride." He gave her a critical look. "Are you all right?"

"I'm okay." She looked at her car and her breath came out in a rush. "My car sure isn't."

"You've been in the restaurant for a while." He nodded to the car's remains. "Any idea on how the fire started?"

She shook her head. "None." She turned her gaze on her car. "My luggage is in the trunk. Do you think it's all burned up?"

He nodded. "Not a chance."

She bit the inside of her lip, having a hard time believing she'd probably lost everything that had come with her. Worst of all was the fact she'd lost her laptop.

"I take it you're from out of town?" he said.

"Yes." She cleared her throat. "I'm from Kansas. I came here to housesit for my friend, Leigh."

"Leigh Monroe?" he asked.

She looked at him with surprise. "Yes."

"I like Leigh," he said. "One of the guys dates her."

"That's right." She should have thought about that. She'd been too stunned over her car being on fire to remember that this firefighter, Cody McBride, might know Leigh.

She started shivering and rubbed her arms before dropping her iPhone again. He picked it up for her, but instead of handing it back to her he put his arm around her shoulders. "You're probably feeling a little shock."

"But nothing happened to me," she said as he guided her toward the back of the fire truck.

"Your car burned up right in front of you along with everything you had inside." He grabbed a blanket from out of the back and put it around her shoulders. "It's normal to have a reaction like this."

She sat on the curb and he crouched beside her and gave her the cell phone he'd picked up.

"I need to call Leigh." Carilyn's hands were shaking as she tried to go into her list of recently dialed numbers to redial Leigh's. "I haven't been able to get hold of her so she doesn't know I'm in town yet."

"Let me help." He steadied the phone for her and Carilyn pressed the number for Leigh.

Carilyn brought the phone up to her ear and heard the call go straight to voicemail. She sighed and disconnected the call. "Leigh must be having problems with her phone or forgot to turn it on."

"After you give your statement to the police and I finish up here, I'll give you a ride to her place and we can see if she's home," he said. "It's not far."

"Thank you." She gave him a little smile. "If it isn't too much trouble."

He got up from his crouched position and held out his hand. "Not at all."

She took his hand. It felt warm and dry and tingles raced through her. She hurried to release his hand when she was standing.

He checked the trunk and sure enough, her suitcases were in ruins, too. A sick feeling made her gut feel like it was churning.

She answered a few more questions about the fire and was unable to give the firefighters or police any idea of how the fire started. Her stomach sickened as she looked once again at the charred carcass that had once been her vehicle.

"Will you be okay here?" he asked. "I'll finish up and then we can head over to Leigh's."

She nodded. "I'm fine."

Cody felt a stirring in his gut as he looked at the beautiful Carilyn Thompson. Something about her had him wanting to comfort her and learn everything he could about her.

He shook the thoughts away and was just about to walk away from Carilyn when a voice came from behind him, calling his name. "McBride."

Cody turned and looked at Bill Johnson. "What's up?" he asked his friend and fellow firefighter.

"You need to check this out." Johnson waved Cody toward the car.

Cody gave a nod to Carilyn then left her sitting on the curb. He went to the car, and looked in the open door. He knelt, studying something on the floorboard. Damn. He hadn't expected this.

Cody frowned as he straightened and faced Johnson. "Has anyone touched it?"

Johnson shook his head. "Exactly as we found it, on the floorboard."

Due to the head fire investigator's accident at one of the arsonist's fires, Cody had taken over as the lead. He had a degree in fire, arson, and explosion investigation, which was now being put to good use.

Cody's features darkened as he looked at the car. They'd already secured the scene and set up a command post so he wasn't concerned about the evidence being disturbed. The firefighters were all professionals and took care not to disrupt the scene more than they'd had to while putting the fire out.

This was most likely another case of arson as it appeared that what Johnson had found was in fact a Barbie doll. It sure as hell looked like it could be. The arsonist had struck three times prior to this, but this was the first car he'd targeted. Every fire had been started differently, from causing an electrical fire in a dress shop, to tampering with natural gas in a home's kitchen, to pouring gasoline around a dance studio and starting it with a match.

Dolls were the only things that connected the crimes. One had been left at each scene at the point of origin, in a small fireproof glass wool tube, so that they were not burned beyond recognition.

This however, was the first time they'd found what appeared to be a doll with no tube protecting it. If it was a doll, they were fortunate it hadn't been burnt completely. The police hadn't released the information about the arsonist's signature to the public so it couldn't be a copycat.

Maybe they'd get lucky and would find someone who had witnessed an individual leaving the scene.

Some time later, after observing and collecting evidence, Cody stood apart from the car and entered his notes on his iPad. He moved his gaze from the tablet to the car, to study what was left of the vehicle. He pictured the crime in his mind. Someone had broken the passenger side window, which hadn't been visible from where Carilyn had been standing when she watched her car burn.

A homemade incendiary device had been dropped through the broken window, landing on the passenger seat. A Barbie doll had been thrown onto the driver's side floorboard. The doll should have completely melted, but the fire hadn't come close to it. The heat had been enough to make it almost unrecognizable, though. Almost. Part of the doll's hair had survived and was clearly a vivid red despite the smoke and heat damage.

When he finished, he turned to see Carilyn sitting on the curb again. Earlier he'd noticed her talking with a police officer. Cody would have to ask her a few questions, too.

He walked to where she sat and looked down at her. "No luck, I take it, in getting hold of Leigh."

She shook her head. "Still no answer."

"I'll get you to her house." He held out his hand and she took it. As he helped her to her feet he met her gaze. Damn, but she had the most beautiful green eyes he'd ever seen. He'd always had a thing for redheads and her hair was a pretty shade of red-gold.

Carilyn pulled her hand away from his and he reluctantly let it go. He'd liked the feel of her hand in his.

She looked up at him. "You don't need to take me to Leigh's. I know you're busy."

"It will only take a few minutes." He offered her a smile. "I want to make sure she's there."

"Okay." Carilyn nodded and then walked to his truck with him.

CHAPTER 2

Still too stunned to think clearly, Carilyn climbed into Cody's truck as he held the door open for her. She was careful not to let her skirt slide up. She buckled her seatbelt then clutched her purse to her belly. It was the only thing that hadn't burned up in the fire because she'd taken it with her into the café.

Cody jogged around the truck and climbed in on the driver's side. He jammed the key in the ignition and glanced at Carilyn. "Are you sure you're all right?"

She managed a little smile. "Considering my car is fried, my laptop and belongings are history, and I am now minus transportation, I'm okay."

He started the truck. "The fact that you weren't in the car at the time is a damned good thing."

She let her breath out. "Yes, there's that."

He maneuvered the truck through the crowd of emergency vehicles. "This may seem like an odd question, but would you have had a doll of any kind in your vehicle?"

Carilyn frowned. "No. Why?"

Cody's brow furrowed. "The object that Johnson showed me may be a burnt Barbie doll."

"I don't have Barbie dolls." A queer feeling stirred in her belly. "They found one in my car?"

"I'm not certain." Cody gave her a reassuring look. "It probably wasn't one, but I have to ask."

Her stomach churned. "Could it have been arson?"

"If it has anything to do with ongoing cases, I can't discuss it. Not yet." He glanced from the road to her. "I don't even know if that's what the object was."

The churning in her stomach started to heat as anger rose through her. "Why would anyone burn up my car? Have other cars been set on fire, too?"

"Other cars, no." His gaze was on the road again. "Like I said, we can't be sure what the object was. I promise to keep you informed as we investigate."

She was certain he wasn't going to say anything else about it, so she looked out the window at the passing town.

"You look familiar to me." He drew her attention back to him and flashed her a quick smile. "And that's not a come-on."

Too bad it wasn't, she thought but said, "I'm from Kansas. I've never been here before."

"I could swear I've seen you." He looked thoughtful. "Are you visiting or moving to Prescott?"

"Visiting." She pushed curls out of her face and realized most of her ponytail had fallen out. "And housesitting while Leigh's gone."

"That's right." He kept his eyes on the road. "Mike said she'll be out of town for awhile."

"Leigh will be gone a month." Carilyn pulled her hair back with both hands and fixed her ponytail. "She'll be touring Europe with a choir group that she sings with."

"Sounds like a good time." Cody glanced at her before looking back at the street. "My brother, Clint, left Prescott and lived in Europe for a few years before moving to Argentina. He was gone for several years and just came home to stay some six months ago."

"He must have liked it there to be gone for so long," Carilyn said.

Cody shrugged. "He was running from his past, but he finally grew up." Cody pulled up to a stoplight. "How do you know Leigh?"

"We were sorority sisters at the University of Kansas." Carilyn smiled as she thought back about those days. "We've kept in touch and have gone on vacations together. Somehow I never made it here until now."

"Leigh is a great gal." The light changed from red to green and Cody started driving again. He gave her a quick grin. "I bet the pair of you have a few crazy stories to tell."

Carilyn grinned back. "We certainly do."

He glanced from the road to her. "I'd like to hear them some time."

For some reason, she found herself wanting to tell him about every one of their stories.

He turned the truck into a neighborhood with tall shady trees and houses that looked to be at least thirty or forty years old. "Leigh lives down this street."

"That was fast." Carilyn watched the houses pass by until they pulled up to a white home with navy blue trim.

Cody parked the truck in front of the home that had an immaculate lawn and trimmed hedges along with towering shade trees. "I'll walk you to the door."

She opened the truck's passenger side door, unsure of how to climb out and keep her short jean skirt from sliding up. Before she could make up her mind, Cody was there, and he held out his hand. With his help she managed to get out of the truck, but still felt embarrassed when her skirt slid higher on her thighs—as if it hadn't been short enough already.

When she was out of the truck, he walked with her on the stone pavers to the house. Carilyn rang the doorbell. At first she didn't think anyone was home, but then she heard the bolt lock slide.

The next thing she knew, Leigh had the door open and her blue eyes lit up with delight when she saw Carilyn on the doorstep.

"Cari!" Leigh hugged Carilyn. "It's so good to see you."

"I'm excited to see you, too." Carilyn grinned as Leigh drew back. "It's been too long."

Leigh cocked her head, her blonde hair falling over her shoulder as she held Carilyn by her upper arms. "Something's happened." She frowned. "And you smell like smoke."

"I'm all right." Carilyn gave a little smile. "I'll tell you all about it."

For the first time, Leigh seemed to realize that Cody was standing nearby. "Cody." She gave him a quick hug. "You look like hell and you smell even more like smoke than Cari does."

Cody braced one hand on the doorframe. "It's good to see you, too." A spark of amusement was in his eyes.

"Don't think I'm not pleased to see you, but why are you here?" Leigh looked from Cody to Carilyn. "What's going on?"

Carilyn sighed. "My car caught fire. Cody was there and helped put it out."

"Oh, my God." Leigh's blue eyes widened. "Your car caught fire?" She looked at the street, her gaze resting on Cody's truck before she looked to Carilyn. "And Cody gave you a ride here?"

"Yes." Carilyn glanced at Cody. "He happened to be eating at the café where my car burned up."

"That's crazy." Leigh shook her head. "Come inside and we'll talk."

"I've got to get back to the fire station." Cody smiled at Carilyn. "It was nice to meet you."

Carilyn found herself wanting Cody to stay and she mentally shook her head. "Thank you for everything."

His gaze rested on Carilyn and he looked like he wanted to say something but thought better of it. When he did speak, he said, "I might need to talk with you again about your car."

She nodded. "Leigh has my number and I also gave it to the police when they took my statement."

"See you, Leigh." He touched the brim of his ball cap as his gaze rested on Carilyn. "Here's to the rest of the day going much better."

Carilyn's heart pounded a little faster at the look in his brown eyes. Then he turned and headed back down the stone pavers to the sidewalk, then around to the driver's side of his truck. Both Leigh and Carilyn watched him as he drove off.

"Wow, he's got it bad for you," Leigh said when she turned back to Carilyn.

Puzzled, Carilyn looked at Leigh. "What?"

Leigh grinned as she pushed the front door all the way open. "You had smooth Cody McBride tongue-tied."

"What are you talking about?" Carilyn stepped past Leigh, into the house.

Leigh followed and closed the door behind them. "Cody never has a problem talking with the ladies from what I've seen. He's easy-going and fun, and women hang off his every word."

"So he's a real ladies' man?" Carilyn asked, a little disappointed.

"Not in the go-out-with-anything-in-a-skirt sense." Leigh gave an amused smile. "Just that women want him without him even trying."

Carilyn's sense of disappointment vanished. "He seems like a nice guy."

"He's a *great* guy." Leigh smiled. "And I seriously think he's got the hots for you."

"Yeah, right." Carilyn rolled her eyes. "Even if he did, I'm only going to be here a month." She moved her attention to the living room. "Your home is gorgeous, Leigh."

"You might be inclined to stay," Leigh said with a laugh, ignoring Carilyn's attempt to change the subject.

"Not happening." Although she was single now that Sam had left her to join the Peace Corps, and her mother and stepfather had retired in Florida… There wasn't much tying Carilyn to Kansas anymore.

Leigh put her hand on Carilyn's arm. "How's everything with your anxiety?" Leigh asked quietly. "This car fire didn't trigger anything, did it?"

"No." Carilyn shook her head. "I've made a lot of progress and I haven't had a panic attack in well over a year now."

"Good." Leigh gave Carilyn a quick hug. "It's so great to see you."

"I'm happy to be here," Carilyn said with a smile. She turned and stepped from the rug in front of the door onto the tiled floor. "I love how you've decorated."

"It's taken a lot of remodeling to get it the way I want it." Leigh's blonde hair swung about her shoulders as she turned and headed toward an archway. "Come on and I'll show you the place and then we'll sit down and you can tell me what happened to your car."

Leigh had beautiful antique furniture in every room. She always wanted Carilyn to go antiquing with her, wherever they traveled.

As they walked through the living room, Carilyn spotted a photograph of herself, Leigh, and their friend Misha from their sorority days. Carilyn laughed. "I have this same photo, framed and in my bedroom."

With a smile, Leigh said, "It's my favorite of the three of us."

After Leigh had given the tour of the house, she led Carilyn to the kitchen. Leigh had a thing for roosters and chickens in her kitchen décor.

"Coffee?" Leigh turned on her Keurig. "I'm dying for a cup."

"I'd love some." Carilyn held back a yawn that suddenly came on. "I could use a little stimulation. It was a long drive out here."

Leigh offered Carilyn a choice of flavored coffee and used the individual serving cups to make Carilyn a cup of Belgium chocolate and butter toffee for herself.

"I bought ice cream." Leigh set the cups of coffee on the table before heading for the freezer.

"Chocolate?" Carilyn asked hopefully.

"Do you even have to ask?" Leigh took a carton of dark chocolate ice cream from the freezer and grabbed an ice cream scoop out of a drawer. She told Carilyn where to find the dessert bowls and spoons.

Carilyn set the dishes and silverware on the kitchen table then took a seat. Still standing, Leigh put two big scoops of ice cream into each of their bowls.

When she'd seated herself, Leigh grabbed a spoon. Carilyn took a bite and gave a blissful smile. "I needed this."

"I'll bet." Leigh dug her own spoon into her chocolate ice cream. "Okay, tell me about your car."

Carilyn sighed. "I arrived two hours early and couldn't get hold of you so I went to a café called the Hummingbird."

Leigh frowned as she picked up her cup of coffee. "You called?"

Carilyn nodded. "Several times."

"My phone never rang." She set down her coffee to dig in her pocket then pulled out a cell phone. When she looked at it she shook her head. "Damn, it's dead. Forgot to charge it." She set it on the table. "You could have come straight here."

"I probably would have eventually," Carilyn said. "I just didn't want to drop in when you weren't expecting me."

Leigh brushed her comment away with her hand. "You didn't need to wait. You should have come on over."

Carilyn took a drink of her coffee then shrugged. "Maybe it was a good thing so that my car didn't catch fire right in front of your house." She gritted her teeth. "I lost my laptop. I'm going to have to build everything from the ground up."

"I'm sorry, Cari." Leigh frowned. "Did you have everything backed up? Or was your backup in the car, too?"

"Everything is backed up." Carilyn nodded. "I keep everything on an off-site server. It'll take some time to download everything and get it set up, but I'm grateful I took care of that before I left."

"Thank goodness," Leigh said.

Carilyn set the cup down and absently ran her finger around the rim. "I think the firefighters found something in the car that makes them think it could be arson."

Leigh's eyes widened. "Arson?"

With a nod, Carilyn said, "Not officially." She explained to Leigh about the object, that Cody had asked her if she had Barbie dolls, and how he wouldn't talk with her about it. "Something to do with ongoing investigations. He said he wasn't even sure the object was a Barbie."

"That's scary." Leigh was frowning. "I haven't heard of any cars catching on fire before."

Carilyn's gaze narrowed. "But you've heard of other fires?"

A light dawned in Leigh's eyes. "There have been some suspicious fires around Prescott over the past couple of months. Three that I know of."

A shiver trailed Carilyn's spine. "Were Barbies involved?"

"I haven't heard anything about dolls being involved." Leigh appeared to be thinking it over. "Maybe it's one of those inside clues like you see on crime shows that isn't made public."

Carilyn looked down into her coffee mug. "Maybe so…"

"So tell me everything you are able to," Leigh said, drawing Carilyn's attention to her.

"Not really much to tell beyond that." Carilyn spooned some of her ice cream. "Went into the café and had a bite to eat, came out and the car was smoking and then burning. Like I mentioned earlier, Cody happened to be eating at the restaurant the same time I was, and apparently came out on my heels." She shook her head. "One moment I was trying to dial 9-1-1 and the next he was rushing by and calling the fire department on his radio."

"Nothing like being rescued by a sexy firefighter." Leigh smiled. "Speaking of sexy firefighters, I don't suppose you met my boyfriend. His name is Mike Lawson."

"I was in a little bit of shock, so I'm not sure if he was there," Carilyn said.

"I'll introduce you to him." Leigh ate another bite before she said, "I'm going to make a batch of cookies and we can take them to the fire department before I leave for Europe. I usually bake the guys something once or twice a month."

"You always did like cooking and baking." Carilyn raised her spoon. "You were the best cook in the whole sorority."

With a laugh, Leigh said, "That's probably how I got in to begin with."

Carilyn grinned. "Not only that, but it was because you made the best homemade ice cream ever."

"I knew it." Leigh waved her spoon. "It was always about the goodies."

Carilyn set her own spoon in her bowl and said more seriously, "It's really good to see you."

"It's good to see you, too, Cari." Leigh gave Carilyn a teasing look. "Now to find a way to get you to stay. I think I'll have a talk with Cody McBride."

"Don't you dare," Carilyn said. "Besides, I'm tired of men."

"Sam hurt you that badly?" Leigh asked quietly.

Carilyn paused to consider. "I loved Sam and still do…but it's a friendly love, nothing more. It was a shock when he told me he was going into the Peace Corps." She sighed as she thought about the last couple of years. "I miss him terribly, but I'm moving on with my life. We'll always be good friends, it just won't be what I thought it would."

"Well, if you're moving on, I know just the cowboy fireman for you." Leigh had a gleam in her eyes.

"Cowboy fireman, huh?" Carilyn smiled. "And I thought he was sexy as a firefighter. Now that I know he's a cowboy too, that changes everything." As the gleam brightened in Leigh's eyes, Carilyn held up her hands in a "whoa" motion. "I was just kidding."

"Ha!" Leigh's grin was wicked. "Behind every joke is a grain of truth."

"Not this time." But even as Carilyn shook her head, she couldn't help thinking of the incredibly sexy firefighter/cowboy. Despite what she'd said to Leigh, she couldn't deny that she really might like to get to know him better.

CHAPTER 3

On the trip back to the firehouse, Cody kept thinking about Carilyn and how much he was attracted to her. It had been a long time since he'd had such a strong reaction to meeting a woman—hell, he didn't remember ever feeling this attracted to anyone. She was the kind of woman a man wouldn't be able to keep his hands off of once he had her.

Damn, she was cute with her fiery red hair, clear green eyes, and that sprinkling of freckles across her nose. From what he'd seen of her, she had a sweet personality and he had a feeling she was a kind and generous person—he was usually right on with first impressions. She had also handled all that had happened well, considering her car had been torched and her belongings destroyed in the fire.

He pictured the moment the women had gotten together. From the enthusiastic way she and Leigh had greeted each other, it was obvious they were very close. Now why did Carilyn look so familiar to him when she'd never been to Prescott? He didn't forget faces. It was going to drive him crazy until he figured it out.

He'd wanted to ask her out, but had found himself tongue-tied, something he'd rarely experienced with the opposite sex. The only other time he could remember was when he'd asked Mindy Hoffer to the senior prom—and that had been a very long time ago.

If given a second chance with Carilyn, he hoped he'd have the balls to ask her out. Why the hell he felt like a love-struck teenager around her, he had no idea.

When he arrived at the fire station, Cody took a quick shower and put on clean clothes. He headed out to the bay while lost in his thoughts. He had a few things to take care of and he always took care of things when they needed to be done.

Mike Lawson walked into the station just as Cody was finishing checking his turnout gear.

"Hey, Lawson," Cody called out, catching the other firefighter's attention.

Mike gave a nod and headed in Cody's direction. "What's up?"

"Saw Leigh earlier." Cody hung his helmet on its hook above his other gear.

"I heard." Mike grinned. "She mentioned that she thought you might have a thing for the gal who's going to be housesitting for her."

Feeling a little sheepish, Cody shook his head. "That obvious, huh?"

Mike hooked his thumbs in his front pockets. "Leigh thought so."

"How about meeting at the Highlander for drinks this Friday night? Bring Leigh." Cody braced one hand on the fire truck. "I'm off that day."

"I'll arrange it." With an amused look, Mike added, "And tell Leigh to bring her friend, right?"

Cody grinned. "You've got it."

"Tell me about the car fire." Mike sobered as he changed the subject. "Leigh had the impression from her friend that it could be arson."

Cody gave Mike the details. "Looks like it could be the same bastard," Cody said as he finished.

Mike's expression turned hard as Cody spoke. "We'll get him," Mike said, determination in his voice.

Cody nodded. "You're damned right we will." He thought about it a moment as he raised his ball cap and pushed his fingers through his hair. "So far we don't have a motive and the only consistent thing between all of the fires is the fact that a doll was left at the point of origin."

Mike nodded. "That's not enough."

Cody set the cap back on his head. "It sure as hell isn't. Damn, but we've got to find him before someone gets killed."

It wasn't until Mike had left that Cody finally remembered where he'd seen Carilyn before. The last time he'd been in Leigh's home he had seen a photograph with her, Leigh, and another woman. Even then he'd thought she was cute.

He shook his head. At least that mystery was solved.

As he left his gear and the truck behind to head from the garage into the fire station, he came to a complete stop as a thought occurred to him. All four businesses and homes had belonged to women. All of the Barbie dolls had different colored hair and the different shades matched each woman's own hair. A blonde woman owned the dress shop, the dance studio was owned by a brunette, the home was owned by a woman with black hair, and then the redheaded Carilyn owned the car.

Why hadn't he seen it before? It had been the red-haired doll, whose hair matched Carilyn's, which had given him the new piece to the puzzle.

He frowned at the implications. The arsonist might hate women and he might be targeting women in general. Or he could be fixated on each woman involved.

Anger burned inside him. The sonofabitch, preying on women.

Cody pushed away any thoughts that what he'd come up with could be coincidence. His gut told him that dolls with hair matching each woman was no damned coincidence. The fact that each woman was beautiful was probably no coincidence, too.

Instead of heading into the common room, he went into the office and seated himself in the office chair in front of the large screen computer monitor. After entering his password on the keyboard, he opened files for all four victims and arranged them on the screen so that he could see them all at once. The notes for Carilyn's case were already there as his iPad had automatically synced the information with the computer system. He skimmed through the contents of each file. From the interviews he'd conducted, there were no other common threads, nothing that could be considered a viable lead.

Why would someone be torching businesses, homes, and vehicles of women? Were they random acts by someone who was a stranger to the women? That was possible considering Carilyn had just rolled into town today and the arsonist likely wouldn't have had the time to establish any kind of relationship with her.

Were these women in danger? Each one would need to be interviewed again to see if anything suspicious had happened since the time each woman's property had been torched. He could be wrong, but he didn't think he was. Not at all.

He pulled his cell phone out of the holster on his belt and dialed his cousin, Detective Reese McBride, who was the lead detective on the case.

"Cody," came Reese's voice when he answered. "It's been all of two days and you already miss me?"

Cody couldn't help a grin, but it faded as he got to the point with Reese. "I need to discuss the arsonist case with you." He explained the theory he'd come up with.

Reese sounded grim when he replied. "I think you've got something there. It's late, so tomorrow we'll arrange to interview all four women again, right away."

"Before someone gets hurt," Cody said. "Or worse."

"Agreed," Reese said.

"I want to go with you," Cody said.

"You've got it," Reese replied. "I'll talk with you tomorrow."

After disconnecting the call, Cody shut down the computer. The chair's wheels rattled as they rolled across tile as he pushed back, away from the desk.

This just might be the break they'd been looking for.

CHAPTER 4

Nathan Morris watched the news with rapt attention. He grinned as the newscaster reported that police officials had no new leads in the arson cases. They did, however, believe that today's car fire was related to the three other arson attacks, but they didn't give any details.

The fact that there was still no mention of the dolls annoyed him, however, and his grin turned into a scowl. It was one of his better ideas. The damned police were keeping that evidence to themselves.

No matter. He'd leak the information himself if he had to. He wanted the world to know how smart he was. Rather than just having kept the information from the public, the police were probably too stupid to have made the connection between the dolls' hair color and the women.

He glanced at a duffle on the floor and the half a dozen or so Barbies and glass wool tubes resting inside. He had plenty of both on hand because he would be searching for more victims

Today he'd screwed up, though, and had almost forgotten the doll. He hadn't had time to stuff the Barbie in the tube and would be lucky if the doll had survived. Although, considering the police believed the arson fires were linked, the doll had probably made it. He never left any other clues behind—he made sure of it.

The redheaded bitch he'd seen today was beautiful. He hadn't actually met her, but she was so fucking gorgeous that she was probably like the rest—a slut who wouldn't give him the time of day. Like the girls in high school had, women still ignored him and refused him. Well, he was getting his revenge now, wasn't he?

Nathan used the remote to turn off the TV and pushed himself out of his recliner and walked to his kitchen table where the scrapbook rested. He started flipping pages, grinning to himself as he did.

Pictures of every woman before and after the fires headed each section. He took pictures of them with his camera phone before researching their property and other belongings. Today was the first time he'd picked a woman and had started a fire without investigating her first. He didn't know why, but hadn't been able to help himself.

He'd printed out color photos of each woman on his printer and taped them into the scrapbook along with pictures of their business or home, or car—before the fire. Then he'd taken pictures as they began to burn before fleeing the scene. He'd printed out news articles he'd looked up online and taped them into the albums, too.

People were starting to get scared, and they should. He wasn't going to stop and he knew the police would never catch him.

He ran his finger over the picture he'd taken of the pretty redhead. He'd managed to avoid her attention and had taken her picture before melting away where she'd never see him.

The news had said the redhead's name was Carilyn Thompson and she was from Kansas. He'd figured as much from her license plate. He'd thought she was probably a new transplant who hadn't had a chance to change her plates. According to the news, though, she was here visiting.

He wondered who she was here to see, where she was now, and how long she'd be here. He'd have to make it his business to find out. He was good at tracking people down. Real good. After all, that was his job—to find people. He wasn't one of the world's best hackers and trackers for nothing.

Money had never been a problem—he'd always made enough to get by. He got paid very well just sitting on his ass at home and working his magic for his clients.

As he closed the scrapbook, he smiled. This was so fucking fun he could barely keep from telling his online buddies about it. Although he covered his tracks so well that he'd never be found, he was still careful. Maybe he *would* tell them. He'd have to give it some thought.

For one brief moment, he thought about his mother. What would she think of what he was doing? Would she even realize it was her fucking fault? All of those cigarette burns had only been the start of what she'd put him through.

He shoved aside the thoughts. This was his time to glory in his brilliance.

Humming to himself, he went into the kitchen and grabbed bread, peanut butter, and grape jelly, along with a carton of milk.

He was famished after his successful day. Being an arsonist of his caliber was like being an artist. It took talent, time, and patience. Not to mention a lot of hard work.

Rather than waiting a few weeks to strike again, he was hungry for more.

And he was hungry for it now.

CHAPTER 5

Thursday morning the kitchen was filled with the smell of fresh baked chocolate chip pecan cookies. Carilyn popped another nugget of cookie dough into her mouth as she spooned globs of it on the baking sheet. "Do you always bake cookies for the firefighters?" she asked Leigh as she set the spoon back in the batter bowl.

Leigh took the filled cookie sheet. "Sometimes I make muffins, Rice Krispy treats, or brownies. Treats easy to cut up that can be picked up with your fingers."

Carilyn grabbed a smaller bowl and plopped a spoonful of chocolate chip cookie dough with no nuts on a new banking sheet. "The guys must love you."

"The feeling is mutual." Leigh opened the oven and slid the sheet she was holding inside before closing it again. "They risk their lives every time they go out on a fire and they don't get paid or appreciated nearly enough." She gave a sly grin. "Besides, it gives me an excuse to see all of those sexy firefighters when I deliver the goodies."

Carilyn laughed as she finished another row. "I hear you about them not being appreciated enough. Firefighters, police officers, and teachers. Three of the most important professions, yet they don't get paid what they're worth."

"Amen." Leigh shut the oven door. "That's the last sheet?"

"Yep." Carilyn scraped the bowl with a rubber spatula and then scooped out the last of the dough to make one more cookie. "This is the batch with no nuts for Cody."

Leigh returned to the table and grabbed the now full sheet and set it beside the stove to wait its turn. "He's going to appreciate that you made cookies just for him."

Carilyn shook her head. "You would have done it anyway."

Leigh grinned. "I'll make a point to tell him that you made those special."

"Stop playing matchmaker." Carilyn shook the rubber spatula at Leigh. "I'm only going to be here a month so there's no point in it."

"Sure there is." Leigh picked up the empty batter bowls from the table and carried them to the sink. "It would be awesome if you moved here, Cari."

"I'm not moving here." Carilyn gave her an exasperated look. "I've lived in Kansas all my life."

"So." Leigh rinsed out the bowls in the sink before putting them in the dishwasher. "You could do with a change. You'll love it here."

Carilyn couldn't help a smile. "Give it up."

A mischievous look was in Leigh's eyes. "Never."

Carilyn helped Leigh put ingredients away in the pantry, clean the counters, and straighten the kitchen as the cookies baked and then cooled.

"I talked with Mike about you not having transportation now that you don't have a vehicle." Leigh leaned against the counter. "So that you don't have to rush out and buy a new car, you can use mine while I'm in Europe. He's going to take me to the airport Saturday."

"Thank you." Carilyn rested one arm on the breakfast bar. "Are you still up for some shopping before we take the cookies to the fire department?" She looked down at the too-long, loose jeans she was wearing that belonged to Leigh who, at five-ten was a good five inches taller than Carilyn and a size bigger. "I can't keep wearing your clothes."

"You look cute with the jeans rolled up like that." Leigh grinned. "But yes, you know I love to shop, whatever the excuse. Plus, maybe I can find a cute dress to take on my trip. You should find something a little dressy too."

Carilyn smiled then sighed. "I need to replace so many things. At least I have a toothbrush," she added. They'd gone to the corner convenience store last night to get a toothbrush and toothpaste. "But replacing my laptop is the most important thing I need to do."

After the cookies were finished baking and had cooled, they headed out to look for a laptop, clothes, and other things that Carilyn would need during her stay in Prescott. It was always fun shopping with Leigh who was bubbly and enthusiastic and had a great eye for style and for what looked great on Carilyn.

When they finished shopping, they unloaded the bags at Leigh's house and put them all into the guest bedroom, including the box with the new laptop. Carilyn sighed. It was going to take forever to upload everything and get it all back into working order so that she'd be ready to work come Monday.

Leigh had a hair appointment scheduled later in the afternoon, so they planned to take the cookies to the fire station and then go to the salon and spa. Carilyn had made an appointment to have a pedicure while Leigh was getting her hair cut.

They grabbed the containers filled with the freshly baked cookies and left. It was a short drive to the firehouse, which did turn out to be close to the location where Carilyn's car had caught fire.

Or was deliberately set on fire, she thought with a frown as they passed by the businesses along the street that hid the parking lot from view.

Leigh parked her Mitsubishi near the fire station and they each grabbed a container of cookies before climbing out of the car. Carilyn's stomach flip-flopped as they walked toward the station. She had no reason to be nervous, but for some reason the thought of seeing Cody again made her feel jittery inside.

The bay was open and the red fire truck gleamed in the afternoon sunlight. A firefighter was polishing the chrome bumper, his back to them. She would know that muscular back anywhere, not to mention that nice ass. Cody's backside was the first thing she'd seen of him yesterday, and she didn't mind getting another look at him from behind.

"Hi, Cody," Leigh called out.

He turned to face them and flashed a grin. "Hey. Good to see both of you." Carilyn's belly flipped again as his gaze met hers. "How are you doing, Carilyn?"

"Good." She managed a smile. "Went shopping earlier so I'll be back in business in no time."

He was holding the rag he'd been using to polish the fire truck and he set it on the big chrome bumper. "I'm glad to hear that."

"We made chocolate chip cookies." Leigh held up the large plastic container she was holding. "Carilyn made some for you with no nuts."

Carilyn wanted to elbow Leigh but she extended the smaller container to Cody.

He smiled at Carilyn and she swore she was going to melt as he took the container from her. "That was really nice of you."

Carilyn returned his smile. "Leigh said you don't like nuts, so it's pure chocolate chips for you."

"Thank you." His gaze held Carilyn's a moment before he nodded toward a door leading into the firehouse. "Come on in. The guys are gonna be happy to see what you've brought."

They headed inside and into the kitchen. Soon Carilyn and Leigh were surrounded by some of the best looking, sexiest men that any woman would feel blessed to be around. There was definitely something hot about a man in uniform, even if the uniform was simply a T-shirt and pants.

"Cari," Leigh called out. She was standing next to an exceptionally handsome sandy-haired man who was just over six feet and had an athletic build. Leigh gestured to Carilyn to come to her. When Carilyn reached her, Leigh said, "Mike, this is my best friend, Carilyn Thompson." She turned to Carilyn. "This is Mike Lawson."

Mike held out his hand and Carilyn took it. "Great to finally meet you," Mike said, a spark in his blue eyes. "Leigh has told me some stories." He shook his head as he released Carilyn's hand.

"Hard to believe someone as cute as you could have gotten into so much trouble."

Leigh gave an impish grin as Carilyn put her hands on her hips. "Just what did you tell him, Leigh?"

"I didn't give away too many of our secrets." Leigh said with a laugh. "Just enough to make him wonder."

"Uh-huh." Carilyn gave a look of mock disapproval. "You know the code."

"Code?" Mike wore an amused expression. "You two have a code?"

Carilyn and Leigh both nodded solemnly. "The girlfriend code," Carilyn said.

Mike laughed. "I'm not sure that's a code I'd want to break."

"Good," Leigh said. "'Cause there's no breaking ours."

Mike put his arm around Leigh's shoulders. "Why don't you two join me and the boys for drinks Friday at the Highlander?"

"Sounds great." Leigh tilted her head and smiled at Mike. She glanced at Carilyn. "Are you up for a little fun tomorrow night?"

Carilyn nodded. "Sure. Why not?" She met Cody's gaze and he smiled at her. As she looked into his warm brown eyes she felt a flutter in her midsection and she wondered if spending time in his company was smart. She could fall for a guy like him and that was not a good idea.

In a matter of moments, she found herself alone with Cody, separate from Leigh and Mike. The other firefighters had polished off the cookies, and after thanking Leigh and Carilyn again, they went back to what they'd been doing.

Carilyn looked at the empty container. "The two dozen cookies sure went fast."

"They always do." Cody inclined his head toward the cabinets. "That's why I put away the cookies you gave me after eating a couple. I'll break them out and share with the guys later."

"Can I ask what you found out about the fire that burned up my car?" Carilyn asked.

He gave a nod in the direction of the kitchen table. "Let's have a seat and I'll tell you what I can. If you don't mind, I have a couple of questions for you, too."

Carilyn walked with him toward the kitchen table and sat across from him. "What can you tell me?" she asked when they were settled.

"I'm sorry to tell you this, but we know it was arson," he said and her skin prickled. "We found an incendiary device and your passenger side window was smashed in."

An angry flush burned beneath her skin. "Why would someone want to burn up my car?"

"It could have been random." Cody held her gaze. "But we don't know for sure what the motive was."

"I can't believe this." She clenched her hands on the tabletop. "It's all so surreal."

"Did you see anyone around when you left the café?" he asked.

She shook her head. "I saw people walking up and down the street, but nothing seemed unusual. No one was near the parking lot when I reached it."

Cody looked thoughtful. "It's possible that one of the pedestrians could have seen someone coming from the direction of the parking lot. We can hope someone will come forward."

"I'd sure like to see him caught, whoever it is." Carilyn ground her teeth. "Do you think this fire is related to any of the others that Leigh told me about?"

"I assume she's talking about the three cases of arson we're investigating now," Cody said. "We do have reason to believe they're related but I can't discuss that yet."

"I understand." She sighed. "Thank you for telling me what you could."

"No problem." He seemed to be studying her. "I promise to let you know what I can as we learn more."

She pushed back her chair as Leigh and Mike approached the table. "Thank you," Carilyn said to Cody. "Leigh has a hair appointment and I'm going to get a pedicure, so I imagine we need to get going."

"Thanks again for the cookies," Cody said as Leigh and Mike reached them.

Carilyn smiled. "You're welcome."

"See you Friday night." Again he looked like he wanted to say something else, but didn't.

Leigh and Carilyn said their goodbyes and headed out of the fire station and to Leigh's car.

"See?" Leigh said with a laugh. "Cody has a thing for you."

Carilyn rolled her eyes. "You're incorrigible."

Leigh grinned. "And I'm right."

Carilyn shook her head. "Well, it doesn't matter if he does because I'm not going there."

But no matter how she tried, she couldn't get the sexy firefighter off her mind.

* * * * *

After Leigh and Carilyn left, Cody went to the fire station's office to find it empty. He booted up the office computer and opened up file folders and documents relating to the arson cases. He pored over information collected from the first three fires, which included interview results, witness statements, scene photographs and videos, insurance inquiries, and forensic testing.

He studied the videos Johnson had taken of each scene. He'd recorded all of the details and had also panned the crowd gathered around, just in case the arsonist was there, perversely watching. No one stood out to Cody, but that didn't mean anything. He'd caught one arsonist in the past using this method and it could happen again.

Cody and Reese had met with two of the victims earlier in the day and neither woman had witnessed anything strange since the fires. They hadn't noticed anyone following them or any individuals around who might make them suspicious.

Janice Barnhart, the third victim and owner of the dress shop, hadn't answered her phone when Reese had tried to contact her and hadn't returned his call. After the first two interviews, Reese and Cody had stopped by her apartment but no one had come to the door when they'd knocked. Reese planned to continue trying to get hold of her, but for all they knew, she may have gone out of town.

For all they knew, the arsonist could have gotten to her.

Cody shook his head. He wasn't about to jump to any conclusions, and that included the possibility that one of the women had been a victim of the arsonist again, only this time not with fire. Still it nagged at him that Janice Barnhart hadn't answered phone calls and hadn't been in her apartment—unless she'd ignored their knocks. It all wasn't sitting well with him.

He'd shared his theory with Reese about the Barbie dolls' hair color, and how each had matched the women who were the victims of the fires. Reese had taken to Cody's theory immediately, and like Cody, Reese was now concerned for the women's safety.

Reese had already had police officers interview employees at local stores that sold Barbies but had come up with nothing that stood out. The arsonist was probably buying his dolls in the Phoenix area, or on the Internet, and that would likely be nearly impossible to provide some kind of clue. If the case didn't break soon, though, the police would have to go public with the Barbie angle.

Frustrated, Cody continued to comb through the reports. He was good at mentally compartmentalizing tasks and other things, and he'd been able to set aside thoughts of Carilyn—for the time being. He had a job to do and he couldn't do it if he was spending his time daydreaming about her.

When he'd finished going through the files, he finally allowed himself to think about Carilyn. She'd been so sweet to bake the cookies with no nuts for him. Images poured into his mind of Carilyn wearing an apron and placing a big tray of cookies on a table as children gathered around…two boys and two girls. He'd always wanted a big family, and four kids would be perfect.

"Whoa." He shook his head, banishing the images from his mind. Where had those thoughts come from? He'd barely met the woman. But, damn. What a woman.

He pushed back his chair and stood. It was getting late and he needed to catch some sleep. He'd be seeing Carilyn tomorrow night and he couldn't wait.

CHAPTER 6

Laughter and music spilled out of the Highlander and into the night as Carilyn and Leigh approached the bar. All day Carilyn had found herself looking forward to tonight despite the fact she knew she shouldn't want to see Cody as much as she did. It was only yesterday afternoon that she'd seen him and it seemed like ages.

As if it might calm her nerves, she brushed her palms down her black skirt that reached mid-thigh. Her entire body felt jittery, as if she'd had half a dozen cups of coffee.

"I'm telling you, Cari," Leigh was saying, "Cody was a little tongue-tied when it came to you."

"I don't think so." Carilyn shook her head. "We talked about the investigation and he wasn't that way at all."

Leigh grinned. "But when it came to you and not some safe topic, he was a lot quieter than normal."

Carilyn rolled her eyes. "You're imagining things."

They reached the front entrance and went inside the Highlander that was hazy with smoke. Carilyn scanned the dim room and saw a bar directly in front of them, two pool tables to the left, a mechanical bull on the right along with a jukebox, and lots of high-tops scattered all over the place. Carilyn had called it a "down and dirty" bar and said that's where the firefighters who weren't on duty hung out every Friday night.

Leigh leaned close and spoke next to Carilyn's ear to be heard over the music and the crack of billiards. "I hear there's poker in the back, invitation only."

Carilyn spotted Cody leaning up against the bar, watching her, and for a moment she lost all sense of rational thought. Something swooped in her belly as she got a good look at him. He wore a western shirt with the sleeves rolled up to his elbows, Wrangler jeans, and brown boots, along with a Stetson. He looked every bit the cowboy that Leigh had said he was.

"Damn, he's hot," Carilyn said before she could catch herself.

Leigh gave a laugh. "I knew you were developing a thing for him."

Carilyn glanced at Leigh. "Am not."

Leigh nodded. "Are too."

Before Carilyn knew it, she and Leigh had reached Cody. She realized for the first time that Mike was there, too, and he was giving Leigh a kiss.

"Hi." Carilyn smiled at Cody.

His gaze held hers. "You look great, Carilyn."

"Thank you." She felt both pleased and self-conscious at once in the black silky blouse that scooped low in the front and dipped down in the back. She and Leigh had picked it out at a great dress shop they'd shopped at yesterday.

Leigh was clearly busy talking with Mike, so Carilyn focused on Cody. No doubt Leigh was making a point of giving Cody and Carilyn time to talk.

Carilyn's gaze drifted around the room and she noticed men throwing darts at a dartboard near the pool tables where both men and women shot pool. She looked back at Cody. "So this is where the firefighters hang out?"

"A lot of the guys come here to blow off steam on a Friday night." He leaned one elbow on the bar. "What would you like to drink?"

"Rum and Coke." She watched him as he turned to the bar, caught the bartender's attention, and ordered her drink.

She started to pull her wallet out of her purse but he shook his head. "I'm buying tonight."

"You don't have to do that," she said. "I can pay my own way."

He put his hand over hers that still held the wallet. His touch sent fire racing through her and set her heart to pounding. "I insist," he said.

She dropped her wallet back into her purse. From the look in his eyes, it was a battle she wasn't going to win with this cowboy. "All right. Thank you."

When the drink arrived she was glad to have something to hold. After a few swallows of her rum and Coke, the drink seemed to steady her and make her feel less nervous around Cody. She noticed that he drank a Rolling Rock beer as he lifted it to his lips.

Laughter and shouts came from the direction of the mechanical bull and she glanced to see a cowboy riding the beast. The bull jerked hard and the cowboy went flying. People gathered around laughed and shouted as another cowboy helped up the first cowboy.

She looked at Cody. "Have you ever ridden that thing?"

He nodded. "My older cousin, Creed McBride, was a professional bull rider and retired not too long ago. When I was a kid I looked up to him and wanted to do everything he did, so he taught me to ride." He grinned. "Doesn't mean I'm any good, but I can hang on pretty well. Or at least I could—it's been a while."

"I'd like to watch you." Carilyn smiled. "See if you've still got it."

"I'll probably end up on my a—" He corrected himself. "On my butt."

"Sounds like fun to watch." She gave him a wicked grin. "Come on, cowboy. You can make it eight seconds."

He looked amused and set his empty beer bottle on the bar top. "All right. Let's go."

She turned to head toward the bull then felt the heat of his hand on her lower back as he guided her through the busy bar. His touch caused a pleasant warmth to course through her.

When they reached the bull, he wrote his name on a chalkboard, beneath two other names. It wasn't long before it was his turn.

Impulsively she reached up and gave him a kiss on the cheek. "For luck," she said as she drew away.

His sexy grin had her sitting at the melting point again. He winked and left her standing near the railing surrounding the mechanical bull.

She set her rum and Coke on a high-top and then gripped the railing as she watched him step down into the pit and onto the straw-covered mat. He climbed up onto the bull, gripped the rope around the bull's chest and gave a nod to the cowboy manning the controls.

Her heart started beating a little faster and she wondered if she should have goaded him into riding. These things could be dangerous, couldn't they?

The bull started off with a wild spin and a buck but Cody managed to hang on. He held one hand up high as he held the rope with his opposite hand. The crowd cheered and some called out his name. Onlookers gave shouts of encouragement or taunted him, all in good fun.

Cody's body jerked in time with the bull and a look of fierce concentration was on his handsome features. She glanced at the digital clock counting the seconds. Five…six…seven… Right at the seven-second mark, Cody went flying. He landed on his ass but easily rolled to his feet. Somehow his cowboy hat had managed to stay on his head.

"Close," she said when he reached her.

He shook his head but was smiling. "Close doesn't cut it in bull riding."

"Getting old," came a voice from behind her.

Cody grinned as he looked at the man who'd spoken and Carilyn looked to see a handsome cowboy joining them. Like Cody, the man was over six feet, had light brown hair, square features, but had intense blue eyes where Cody's were brown. The man looked hardened, like someone who had witnessed a lot, and a lot of that not good.

"Reese, this is Carilyn Thompson," Cody said as he gave a nod toward her. "Carilyn, this is my cousin, Detective Reese McBride."

"Ms. Thompson." Reese held out his free hand to Carilyn and she took it. A beer bottle was in his opposite hand. "My partner, Detective Petrova, took your statement at the scene."

"It's nice to meet you, Detective McBride." Carilyn smiled as they released hands. "I liked your partner. She has good bedside, er rather curbside, manners."

Reese's expression relaxed and the corner of his mouth tipped up in a grin. "I'll be sure and tell her that." He looked a little more serious. "How've you been since the fire?"

She shrugged. "Fine, considering."

He nodded. "Notice anything odd since the fire?"

She tipped her head to the side. "Not that I can recall. Why?"

"Just a little follow-up." He held the beer bottle as if prepared to take a swig. "I'll be calling you to set up a time to go over a few things."

"Okay," she said.

"But for now it's time for you to loosen up, Reese," Cody said with a grin. "By that beer in your hand I'd say you're not here to work."

"Sometimes it's hard to shake off the job." Reese smiled, his features relaxing again. "I'll talk with you later, Ms. Thompson," he said to Carilyn. To Cody he said, "Work on that grip."

Cody saluted Reese who gave a nod to Carilyn before he slipped into the crowd and disappeared from sight.

She picked up her rum and Coke from off the high-top she'd set it on and took a sip.

"Did you get everything you needed when you went shopping with Leigh?" he asked.

Carilyn lowered her glass. "Pretty much. The most important thing was a new laptop, which I'm going to have to set up so that I can get to work when Leigh takes off for Europe."

"What kind of work do you do?" he asked.

"I'm what you call a geek." She smiled. "I'm a computer programmer." She didn't mention that she was also a hacker—but for the good guys.

He raised his eyebrows. "You don't look like the geeky type to me."

She grinned. "And what's a geeky type supposed to look like?"

He returned her grin. "I guess I'm just going to have to change my way of thinking if geeks are as beautiful as you."

She felt her face warm and was glad the bar was dim so that he couldn't see her blush.

"So what do you do?" he asked.

"I contract for the government." She set her now empty glass down. "I'm working on a big project right now that I can't talk about."

"A mystery woman," he said.

Desperate to change the subject from herself, she decided to turn the tables on him. "So you're not only a firefighter, but a cowboy, too?"

He nodded. "I have a little spread that I inherited from my parents."

"How do you have time to work on it?" She tilted her head to the side. "With the kind of hours and schedule a firefighter works, doesn't that make it difficult?"

"It can." He pushed the brim of his hat up a little with one finger. "I used to hire 4-H kids and all of them did a good job. But now I have a ranch hand who handles things when I'm gone. Tom is semi-retired and lives on a place not too far from mine so he's available when I need him. It's easier having him than juggling the kids."

"I've never been on a ranch." Carilyn wondered how close real ranches were to what was portrayed in the movies.

"I'll have to show you around my place," he said. "If you don't have anything planned tomorrow, you could come on over if you'd like."

Carilyn hesitated. Was this getting too close to going out on a date with the man? She really did want to go out on a ranch. "Okay," she said. "Mike is giving Leigh a ride to the airport around five in the morning so I'm free for the day. She's leaving her car for me to drive while she's gone."

"Great." He smiled. "I'll give you directions. Smart phones aren't always so smart once you head away from town."

She found herself brushing down her skirt with her palms for something to do with her hands. "What time?"

"How about ten?" he said. "I can take you riding."

"Riding?" She felt a twinge in her belly. "I've never been on a horse."

"I'll let you ride one of my gentlest horses," he said. "She's a real sweetheart."

She gave him a nervous smile. "I guess I'll trust you on that."

"You can definitely trust me." He inclined his head toward the bar. "Let's get another drink."

"All right," she said, at the same time wondering what happened to her insistence to Leigh and herself that she should keep her distance from Cody. She certainly wasn't doing a very good job of it.

When they were seated at the bar and after Cody had ordered drinks for both of them, he rested one arm on the bar top as he looked at her. "Do you have family in Kansas?" he asked.

She shook her head. "Not anymore. My mom and stepdad retired and moved to Florida." She hesitated and a sharp ache stabbed her gut like it always did when she mentioned her father. "My birth father might be there, but it's hard to count him as family since he abandoned my mom and me when I was very young."

"No cousins or any other family there?" Cody asked.

"All of my relatives live in Indiana." Carilyn ran her fingers up and down her rum and Coke glass. "Mom ran away to Kansas with my birth father when she was just seventeen. When my father left us, she didn't have enough money to move back to Indiana and she refused to ask family for help. So we stayed. By the time she could afford to move she'd met my stepdad and his roots run deep in Kansas."

Cody looked thoughtful. "How is your relationship with your stepdad?"

Carilyn smiled. "George is like a father to me. Much more so than my birth father." She cocked her head to the side. "What about you? Do you have much family here? I met your cousin and you mentioned a brother."

"My parents passed away some time ago," Cody said. "But I have a boatload of cousins, aunts, and uncles in the Prescott Valley. The McBride clan is one of the biggest and oldest families in the area."

"I take it your reunions are pretty wild?" Carilyn said.

He laughed. "You could say that."

Carilyn shifted on her seat. "I'd bet you have some stories to tell."

"You have no idea." He grinned. "Do you have anything planned while you're here?"

"I haven't made any plans yet." She pushed a loose curl from her face. "I do want to go to Sedona sometime. I hear there's a great dress shop there."

His lips twitched. "Couldn't vouch for that, but I can tell you that Sedona has one of the best fudge shops anywhere. The only fudge I've had that's better is Leigh's."

"You're a big fan of fudge, I take it," she said. "Plain with no nuts, right?"

"You've got it," he said. "You could say I'm a purist."

She laughed. "I'll have to try some when I go."

"If you'd like someone to go along, I'd be glad to take you," he said.

Something tickled her insides as she met his gaze. "I'd like that." She found herself saying the words before she could stop herself. She'd already made plans to go to his ranch, and now Sedona, too?

He smiled. "I'm looking forward to it."

She suddenly felt jittery and wondered why she would feel nervous now. "I should find Leigh." She let her gaze drift over the room but didn't see her friend.

"It's possible she went outside with Mike," Cody said. "It would be easier to hear out there."

She turned back to him. "I'm only going to be here a month," she found herself saying.

He nodded. "You might as well enjoy yourself while you're here." He gave a little grin. "Who knows? You might decide to stay."

"I don't think so." She couldn't help returning his smile. "You and Leigh don't give up easily though, do you."

"Nope." He shifted his elbow on the bar. "Do you have anyone back in Kansas?"

"If you mean a boyfriend, then no." She shook her head. "My long-time boyfriend broke it off and went into the Peace Corps a few months ago."

"That must have been a tough thing to go through," Cody said.

She considered it for a moment. "It was unexpected and it wasn't easy, but I've moved on."

Cody raised his beer bottle. "Are you still friends with your ex?"

"He's a good guy," she said as Cody took a drink of his beer. "We'll always be friends."

Carilyn started to ask him if he had any girlfriends, but Leigh's cheery voice drew Carilyn's and Cody's attention.

"I've got an early flight so I need to head home and get to bed," Leigh said.

Carilyn slid off her barstool. "I'm ready."

Cody got up from his stool and pulled a cell phone from a holster on his belt. "Why don't you give me your number and I'll text you directions in the morning?"

"Directions?" Leigh looked intrigued.

Carilyn knew she was in for a grilling once they got out of the bar. "Cody invited me to his ranch tomorrow. I've never been on a ranch."

Leigh gave a wide smile. "That's awesome."

Carilyn wanted to elbow Leigh, who looked tremendously pleased, but instead Carilyn turned her attention back to Cody and rattled off her phone number, which he entered into his phone contacts.

He shoved the phone back into his holster. "See you tomorrow morning."

"See you," Carilyn said before she turned and walked out the door with Leigh.

As they headed into the cool night, Leigh put her hand on Carilyn's arm and squeezed. "I knew you two would get together."

Carilyn shook her head. "I'm just going to his ranch." She wasn't ready to tell her friend that she'd said she'd go to Sedona with him, too. Leigh would be unbearably excited about it.

"Well it's a great start," Leigh said with satisfaction.

A start to what? Carilyn wondered. Certainly not a relationship—that wasn't going to happen.

CHAPTER 7

Leigh and Mike left for the airport before Carilyn woke Saturday morning, and now Carilyn found herself driving to Cody's ranch. It was starting out to be a pretty day with a clear blue sky, not a cloud anywhere to be seen.

When the text came in that morning from Cody with his address and directions, Carilyn had felt an inexplicable burst of excitement to see a message from him. Well, maybe it was explainable—but she really did know better.

If she knew better, why was she driving to Cody's ranch this very minute?

She shook her head. The fact was that she was undeniably attracted to him, and seeing him like this was a dangerous road to follow when she would only be here for a month.

It isn't a problem, she told herself. She could handle this. Sure she could.

Fifteen minutes after leaving town, she arrived at a mailbox with C. McBRIDE stenciled on it. She'd seen two other mailboxes with the same last name, but this was the only one resting on a green pole like he'd mentioned in the directions.

She turned onto the drive that the mailbox marked and Leigh's car jostled and vibrated as it crossed over a cattle guard and down the bumpy dirt road.

The closer Carilyn got to the ranch at the end of the road, the harder she clenched the steering wheel. *Breathe*, she told herself. *Just relax.* Easier said than done.

She crossed another cattle guard as she looked at the sprawling ranch house, the large barn, and what looked like a storage shed. Corrals were behind and to the side of the barn and three horses were inside one of the corrals. Reddish-brown cows with white faces were on the other side of the fence in a pasture covered with green grass.

When she pulled up to the house and parked, the front door of the house opened and Cody stepped through the doorway. Her heart pounded a little faster when she saw his sexy smile and she watched his easy stride toward the car. She turned off the car and brushed her sweaty palms on her jeans before pulling the keys out of the ignition. She'd just leave her purse in the car—she wasn't going to need it now.

She pushed her long red braid over her shoulder and started to open the car door, but Cody was there before she could and he opened it for her. She climbed out and stuffed the car keys in the front pocket of her jeans as he shut the car door.

"Hi." She smiled at him.

"Welcome to the old homestead," he said with a return smile and a shy hug.

He stepped back and she said, "Thanks for inviting me." She wasn't sure what else to say so she looked at the livestock. "What kind of cows do you have?"

"I have Hereford cattle." He gave a nod in that direction. "Come on and I'll show you around."

"All right." She fell into step beside him. The midmorning sun was warm on her arms that weren't covered by her plain cinnamon-colored T-shirt.

He glanced at her as they walked. "Did you have any problems finding my place?"

She shook her head. "None at all."

They walked up to a pasture fence. The smell of manure was strong—it reminded her of times she'd gone to the state fair as a kid and had looked at the animals.

"I breed to sell to 4-H and FFA kids around the state to raise and show at competitions as well as county fairs and the state fair," Cody said as they stopped in front of the fence. "So my herd is show quality. I also sell steers to individuals who buy for the fresh beef."

"I'm a city girl," she said. "What's the difference between a cow and a steer?"

"A cow is a female who has given birth at least once or twice." He gestured to one of the larger animals, then moved his finger to point to a smaller one. "Heifers are from one to two years old and have never calved.

"Calves are less than ten months old and rely on their mother or a bottle for milk," he continued as he nodded to a pair of calves beside a cow. He moved to a larger animal. "A steer is a castrated male and used primarily for beef."

She nodded. "And bulls are males used for breeding?"

"Yep." He pointed to a larger animal corralled a good distance from the pasture. "That's the bull."

"So you don't refer to a herd as cows," she said.

"That's right," he said. "They're referred to as cattle. A rancher will refer to the number he or she owns as how many head of cattle they have." He nodded toward the herd. "I have twenty-five head right now."

"Why don't they have horns?" she asked.

He looked at her. "Hereford are normally horned, but these are naturally polled through selective breeding."

"Interesting." She smiled. "Learn something new every day."

With a grin he said, "Ready to see the horses?"

She nodded. "You bet."

They approached the corral with the three large animals. "Are you familiar with horses?"

"Not more than that they're horses," she said. "I've never ridden and I couldn't begin to tell you what kind they are."

"All three of my girls are Quarter horses." He gestured to one on the left. "She's a palomino. That refers to her coloring—gold coat and white mane and tail." He nodded toward the other two. "The twins are also Quarter horses but they're sorrels."

"One palomino and two sorrels, all three are Quarter horses," she repeated. "Got it." She looked up at him. "What does sorrel mean?"

They reached the corral and Cody put his hands on the top wooden rail before stepping onto the bottom rail and raising himself up. "It's for their brownish-red coloring."

Carilyn followed his example and climbed up onto the rails. He was somewhere around six-one, a good seven inches taller than her, so he was a good deal higher over the top rail than she was.

He whistled and the horses raised their heads. The palomino started toward them. Cody glanced at Carilyn. "I have a different whistle for each of my girls." When the horse reached them, he stroked her forehead. "This is Dolly."

Carilyn laughed. "With all of that blonde hair, the palomino must be named Dolly after Dolly Parton, right?"

"You've got it." He grinned. "One of the 4-H kids who worked for me named the other two when they were born. The one with white markings is Molly. The other is Holly." He reached into his pocket and pulled out a few green pellets. "Why don't you feed these to Dolly? Let me see your palm." Carilyn did as he told her and he dropped the pellets onto her palm. "Now hold out your hand."

She wrinkled her forehead. "Dolly won't bite?"

He shook his head. "Nope."

Carilyn did as he told her. Dolly snuffled over Carilyn's palm and the horse's velvety muzzle tickled her hand. The horse smelled...horsey. The next thing she knew, the pellets were gone.

"Dolly is so beautiful," Carilyn said as she stroked the mare's forehead. She glanced at the other pair that looked interested in what was going on. "So are your sorrels. Can I feed Holly and Molly, too?"

"You bet." He whistled to the sorrels and they both trotted over to Carilyn and Cody.

Carilyn held out her palm again and Cody gave her a few pellets, which she fed to Molly. "Their muzzles feel so soft." She held out her hand to Cody and he put more pellets on it, which she fed to Holly.

When they had fed all of the pellets to the horses, Cody said, "If you're up for it, I'd like to take you out for a ride." He nodded to the sorrel with the white markings. "You can ride Molly."

She held her hand to her belly. "What if I fall off?"

"I promise, you'll be fine." He inclined his head toward the house. "Let's pack a picnic lunch and then we'll head on out."

She found herself feeling more excited than doubtful and she smiled at him. "Okay. I'm ready to experience ranch life."

"Great." He started toward the house and she walked beside him. "What do you like—roast beef, turkey, or egg salad?"

"Any of those is great," she said, "but if I had to choose one I'd go with egg salad."

The house was cool as they stepped inside. The living room was spacious, with chocolate brown leather sofa and love seat, a recliner in caramel-colored leather, a big wooden rocker, and a large flat-screen TV. Cody hung his hat on a rack by the front door. A guitar case was next to the hat rack.

She glanced from the case to Cody. "Do you play guitar?"

"Yep," he said. "I've been playing since I was a kid."

Carilyn followed him into the kitchen with light oak cabinets, dark granite countertops, and stainless steel appliances. A round oak table with four chairs was in a nook to the right.

She looked around the kitchen. "I like your kitchen."

"Thanks. Just had it remodeled in January." He went to the fridge and ducked inside. In moments he had pulled out condiments, meats, and hard-boiled eggs, along with tomatoes, lettuce, and cheese.

They set about putting several sandwiches together. Carilyn only wanted one egg salad sandwich, but Cody made three different sandwiches for himself. With their picnic lunch, he included Oreo cookies, corn chips, green grapes, and a thermos of iced tea. When they were finished, he packed everything into a saddlebag, including paper plates, paper napkins, and a canteen of water.

"Hold on and I'll be right back," he said.

She nodded and he left the kitchen. When he came back, he was wearing a holster with a revolver in it.

Her brows lifted. "You're carrying a gun?"

He nodded. "You never know out here if you might run into a rattlesnake. These bullets have snake shot in them."

At the mention of rattlesnakes, her eyes widened. "You're worried about snakes?"

"Not really." He walked to the saddlebags and slung them over his shoulder. "But better safe than sorry."

She followed him out of the kitchen. He grabbed his hat off the hat rack and put it on.

As they left the house and walked to the barn, nervous tension settled on her shoulders and she rolled them to try and get rid of it. She was actually going to ride one of those big animals and attempt to stay on it.

Once they were in the barn, Cody set aside the saddlebags and whistled to Molly and Holly, and the sorrel mares trotted into the barn. He haltered Molly and took her to the tack room where he put a thick saddle blanket and saddle on her back. After Molly was taken care of, Cody took Holly out of the pen and saddled her, too.

When Cody was finished, he put the saddlebags on Holly then turned to Carilyn. "I'll help you mount Molly."

Carilyn rubbed her hands on her jeans while she felt a quick burst of nerves, but nodded and went to the horse. Cody instructed her on how to mount the big animal. With his help, from the left side of the horse she put her left foot in the stirrups and swung her right leg over before settling into the saddle. Not very gracefully, but she made it into her seat. It felt strange sitting on a saddle, the huge beast between her legs.

With one hand on the pommel, Carilyn leaned forward and patted the big horse's neck. "That's a good girl, Molly," she murmured before settling back into the saddle.

It felt kind of cool sitting so high up and feeling the horse shift beneath her. The mare's tail swished as she swatted flies off of her large rump. It surprised Carilyn when she realized that her nervousness had vanished to be replaced by excitement.

Cody handed her the reins. "I'll tell you what to do once we take off."

She nodded and tried holding on to the excitement and to remain loose and not uptight. She watched as he mounted his own horse then moved Holly close to Molly.

He instructed her on how to hold the reins and how to get the horse to go in the direction she wanted it to.

"Molly will follow Holly, so you don't need to worry too much about it," Cody said when he finished.

Carilyn fiddled with the end of her braid. "Okay."

When they started out of the barn, her belly swooped again as she felt the horse move beneath her. She gripped the reins tightly but tried to relax at the same time like Cody had instructed her.

They reached the pasture and Cody dismounted and opened the gate. He led both horses through then closed the gate behind them before mounting Holly again.

Carilyn breathed in the fresh air and felt the breeze against her cheeks as they started into the pasture. She felt a sudden high from the cool spring morning and being astride such a majestic animal.

"This is fun." She flashed a smile at Cody. "Thanks for inviting me."

"I'm glad you're enjoying it." He returned her smile. "It's a beautiful day for a ride."

"It is." She tipped her face up to the sun for a moment before looking back to him. "I'll worry about setting up my laptop tomorrow. I was going to do that today, but this is much more fun."

"I imagine it's going to take you a little time to load your new laptop with everything you need," he said.

"It's going to be a pain in the butt." She sighed. "I lost a perfectly good laptop that was less than a year old. Thursday I called to have software overnighted to me that is specialized for the work I do, and it arrived yesterday morning."

"Do you work on weekends?" he asked.

She shrugged as her body rocked in the saddle. "If it's crunch time for a big project, I'll work a lot of overtime. Otherwise I try to keep regular office hours on weekdays. All work and no play is a good combination for a case of burnout, and I do my best to avoid it. Been there, done that."

"Do you enjoy what you do?" he asked.

"Yes." She smiled. "Most of the time."

"I think it's that way with most jobs." He grinned. "I love ranch life, and I enjoy being a firefighter, but it's nice to have a break from each of them at times. Maybe that's why I like both jobs—one gives me a break from the other."

She cocked her head. "But does that mean you're always working with something?"

"I take time off as needed," he said. "Like you said, burnout is a danger if you don't give yourself a break."

"So you enjoy being a firefighter?" she asked.

He nodded. "Yep."

"I imagine it can be hard at times." She thought about the challenges he probably faced. "Not to mention you're constantly putting your life on the line."

"The rewards of the job outweigh the negative." He looked thoughtful. "Saving a life makes up for times when the job can get rough."

Her stomach had settled and she rocked in the saddle in time with Molly's movements as the horses made their way through the grassy pasture. The grass was green, the soil soft enough that the horse's hooves made prints. The air smelled clean and wonderful.

"Have you been getting rain in this area?" she asked.

"We had good rains earlier this week, before you arrived. We were in a drought, but we've now had more rain than normal for this time of year." He adjusted his western hat. "It won't be long until it's summer and the grass turns yellow and the dirt is dry. The rain won't keep up like this."

She let her gaze drift over the land. "It's beautiful out here."

"You can understand why this land would be hard to leave," he said.

As she continued to take in the view, she said, "Yes, I can understand it." She turned to him. "I saw McBrides listed on mailboxes on the way here. So there are a lot of ranchers in the family?"

"Most of the family is in the ranching business." Cody adjusted his Stetson. "Now that our cousins have started having children of their own it's hard keeping track of everyone."

"You mentioned last night that your parents passed away some time ago," Carilyn said.

"Mom died from a ranching accident years ago, when I was pretty young," Cody said. "It's been some time since my father passed away after a long bout with cancer."

"I'm sorry." Carilyn's voice was low, quiet. "What kind of ranching injury did your mom die from? If you don't mind me asking."

"Mom got hooked by a horned bull." Cody looked ahead as he spoke. "That's one reason why I'll only keep polled cattle."

"How awful." Carilyn felt an ache in her chest for Cody. "You said something about a brother, too, who was in Europe for a while."

"My older brother, Clint." Cody glanced at her. "I think I mentioned to you that he took off after his best friend died in a rodeo accident. He came back last summer. This July he's marrying his best friend's kid sister, Ella. She's a real sweetheart and a great artist."

Carilyn tipped her head to the side. "I'd like to see her work."

"She's talented," Cody said. "Her sculptures and pencil drawings are in a Scottsdale art gallery, and she just had a piece commissioned by a large New York City gallery."

While they rode, Cody told her stories of his brother and himself when they were young. "We got our butts whipped for climbing on the roof when we were little. I almost slid completely off the roof and was hanging from the rain gutter when our dad came out of the house. He caught me when I slipped. He was so mad and so relieved."

Carilyn's eyes widened. "He whipped you?"

"A couple of times with a belt." Cody shrugged. "That was how his generation grew up. Beat idiocy out of a kid." He shook his head. "I'd never do that to my children, but my parents came from other times."

"My mom used a wooden spoon." Carilyn's lips twisted into a wry expression. "To this day I don't like wooden spoons."

"How long have your mom and stepdad lived in Florida?" Cody asked.

"They retired a couple of years ago." Carilyn gave a small sigh. "I sure miss them."

"Do you get to see them often?" Cody asked.

"Not often enough," Carilyn said. "Fortunately with my career I can travel and still work, so I go to Florida two or three times a year. I just miss having her close. We always did so much together."

Cody gestured ahead to a small copse of trees. "We'll have lunch there."

"Great." She shifted in her saddle. "I'm getting hungry."

"Can't have that." He clicked his tongue and his horse started to trot.

Molly followed suit and then Carilyn was bouncing in her saddle as the horses trotted toward the trees.

When the reached the copse, Cody brought Holly to a halt, and Molly stopped, too.

Carilyn leaned forward, her hands on the pommel. "It's pretty here."

"I sure think so." Cody dismounted then walked to Carilyn and Molly. "My family moved to Arizona back in the 1880's. That makes me a native and I have to say I love my state."

"I love all of the mountains." Carilyn looked around her. "Where I live, it's flat as flat can be. The mountains are much prettier."

Cody reached her and held up his arms. "I'll help you down."

She let him help her dismount. The moment her feet were on the ground, she found herself standing close to him, their bodies inches away. His hands clasped her waist and her palms rested on his shoulders. She felt the heat of his touch through her T-shirt and beneath her hands. She swallowed as she met his gaze and breathed in his masculine scent.

Her heart pounded as she looked up into his warm brown eyes and his grip tightened, telling her he felt the connection too. She longed to stroke her fingers along the day's growth of stubble on his square jaw, to run her palms down the hard expanse of his chest. Her breath caught in her throat and a thought rattled around in her head... *What am I doing?*

His gaze held hers before she broke the spell and stepped back. Her hands slid off his shoulders and he dropped his own hands from where they had rested on her hips. It seemed like he'd held her several minutes, but it was probably just a matter of seconds.

Feeling awkward with Cody for the first time that day, she looked away and concentrated on looking at bird scuttling across the ground. "That must be a quail," she said as Cody grabbed the saddlebags off of Holly.

"We have a lot of quail out here," he said as it scuttled under a bush. "My mom loved them and we even raised some at one time."

He opened one of the saddlebags and pulled out a plaid blanket. She took it from him to spread it out on a clear place on the ground beneath the trees. They both sat on the blanket and he began taking their lunch out of the saddlebags and placing them on the blanket. He handed her a paper plate.

She took an egg salad sandwich from him and removed it from its plastic baggie. After she took a bite, chewed, and swallowed, she smiled at him. "This has got to be the best egg salad sandwich ever."

He gave an amused smile. "It's the country air. Makes everything taste better."

"I'll say." She slipped her hand into the corn chips, pulled out a handful, and placed them on her paper plate. "Is this the ranch you grew up on?"

He nodded. "From the time I was born. My brother and I inherited it but he signed the ranch over to me when he got back from traveling abroad."

"I live in a small apartment and don't get out of the city much." Carilyn pulled several grapes out of a baggie and set them on her plate. "All of this space is just incredible to me." She looked out at the pasture. "I can see how this land would be inspiring. I like to go to coffee shops to get out of the house and work on my laptop. Might do that in town."

"There's a great bakery in Prescott called Sweet Things," Cody said. "Not too long ago, one of my cousins married the woman who owns it. She has tables and chairs that you can sit in and a big picture window to stare out of."

"Sounds great," Carilyn said. "I'll have to check it out."

She enjoyed talking with Cody. He was so easy to talk with, so comfortable to be around.

Even though they'd been there well over an hour, it seemed that they finished lunch too quickly and it was time to pack up. She helped gather up the trash and stuffed everything into a saddlebag, which he slung over his horse and secured.

When he helped Carilyn mount her horse, she felt a flurry of nervous excitement in her belly. All too soon his hands were no longer on her and he was mounting Holly.

When they set out and Carilyn smiled at the gentle sunny day and her enjoyment of her time with Cody.

As the horses headed back toward the ranch house, Carilyn heard a strange noise, like the rattle of a pressure cooker.

Molly whinnied a loud terrified sound, and reared up on her hind legs.

Carilyn screamed as she lost her grip on the reins.

The next thing she knew, she was flying off the back of the horse.

She hit the ground hard, air whooshing out from her chest. Her head struck something.

Stars blinded her and then everything went black.

CHAPTER 8

Cody's heart thundered as he saw Carilyn being thrown from her horse. At the same time, he un-holstered his pistol and aimed it at the rattlesnake just feet from where Carilyn landed. He pulled the trigger. The snake collapsed as Cody hit it in the head dead-on with the snake shot.

He dismounted Holly in a rush and ran to where Carilyn lay flat on the ground, motionless. As he reached her a breath of relief rushed out of him when she stirred.

She groaned and started to move but put her hand to her head and grimaced.

"Shhh." He crouched beside her, one knee on the ground, and touched her shoulder. "Don't move."

She blinked. Her pupils were dilated and she had a dazed look about her. "What happened?" Her speech came out a little slurred.

"A rattlesnake spooked Molly. You got thrown and you likely have a concussion." He saw blood on the rock behind her head. "You also have a head wound. I'm not sure if you have any other injuries."

"My head hurts." She tried to get up but he lightly but firmly pressed her down by her shoulders.

"Relax the best you can." He let out his breath. "Give me a moment and I'll get the first aid kit."

He went to the saddlebags and from the bottom of one he pulled out a first aid kit and a clean bandana that he kept for working in the heat. When he turned around he frowned when he saw that she was now sitting up. She had one knee bent and she was resting her elbow on it, her forehead in her hand.

When he went to her, he knelt and set the kit aside with the bandana on top of it. "I told you to relax."

"I'm not the best patient." She raised her head and gave him a weak smile. "I just got the wind knocked out of me. I'm okay."

"I'll determine if you're okay." He put the bandana on his thigh and opened the kit. He brought out antiseptic and a cotton pad. "Who's the paramedic here?"

"That's right. Firefighters usually have paramedic training, don't they?" she said.

"Here they do." He took the cotton pad and looked at the back of her head. Her red hair was dark with blood. "I'm going to clean and wrap this before we get you home."

She started to nod and then winced. "Yes, sir."

"If you can move, we'll get you out of here." Where there was one rattlesnake, there could be another if its mate was nearby.

He set about cleaning the dirt out of the wound then put a pad over the laceration. He wrapped the bandana around her head, holding the pad into place.

When he finished, he rested his hand on her shoulder. "How do you feel?"

"Like I just got thrown off a horse and hit my head." She gave a wry expression. "It hurts to talk."

"Then talk as little as possible." He squeezed her shoulder. "How about the rest of you?"

"I can move." She moved her feet and bent her other knee, too. "I think I'll be okay."

"Hold on and I'll get the thermos of water so you can take Tylenol for the pain." He got to his feet. "You're going to need it."

After he gave her the Tylenol and had put away the thermos and the first aid kit, he took a moment to bury what was left of the snake's head and its venomous fangs.

He checked her again. When he was as sure as he could be that all she'd come away with was a laceration to her scalp and a mild to moderate concussion, he brought her up with him, supporting her as she got to her feet.

"You're going to ride with me," he said. "When we get to the ranch, I'm going to take you to the doctor."

"I don't want to go to the doctor," she protested. "I—I'll be okay."

He frowned. "You may be hurt worse than you think you are."

"No." She looked like she was going to cry. "I hate going to see doctors. Please, just let me rest at your house."

He didn't answer as he raised her up and helped her onto Holly so that she was sitting at the front of the saddle.

"I mean it, Cody," she said. "I'll be okay. Promise?"

He looked at her for a long moment. "All right. But if you get worse, I'm taking you. Understand?"

Her chin jutted out as she looked at him stubbornly. With a shake of his head, he boosted himself up and swung his leg over the horse and seated himself behind Carilyn. Their bodies were snug against each other. He whistled to Molly who was standing a good twenty feet away. She trotted closer, but wouldn't go near the snake's body.

He wrapped one arm around Carilyn's waist and handled the reins with his other hand. As they headed toward the ranch house, Molly fell into stride behind Holly.

Carilyn leaned back against him and he liked the way her body felt next to his. This wasn't the way he'd have wanted to get this close to her, but she felt comfortable in his arms.

"You okay?" he asked.

"Yes," she said. "But I don't think I'm going to be playing Jeopardy anytime soon. Having a hard time thinking straight."

"All part of the concussion." He let the horse walk rather than trot to keep the jostling to a minimum. "You're not driving anywhere for at least twenty-four hours."

"I need to set up my laptop in the morning so that I'll be up and running by Monday," she said.

"Honey, you're not going to feel like doing anything that requires brain power." He gripped her more tightly. "You're going to need to make yourself relax, no matter how hard that seems to be."

"I'm not a workaholic," she said. "But I do like to keep on a schedule."

He barely kept himself from nuzzling her hair as he held her. "Sometimes you've got to just give in to the doctor whether you want to or not."

She gave a soft laugh. "If you say so, Dr. McBride."

"I say so." He gauged how far it was back to the house. It was a good twenty-five minutes away from where they were now. "Now do what I said and relax the best you can."

As she settled more fully against him, she sighed. Even though she was injured, his body reacted to her firm bottom against his groin. He ground his teeth, trying to think about something that would get his mind onto other things.

He let her rest and she didn't seem inclined to talk, which was expected after this kind of injury.

"Tell me about growing up on the ranch," she said after a while.

He told her some stories from his childhood, which brought back memories he hadn't thought about in a long while.

Clint and Cody had both been into rodeo from a young age, but Clint had been the one who excelled at it and had gone on to be a champion when they were out of their teens. Clint had left at the height of his career. Cody had focused on ranching before he decided to go to college to get a degree and get on with the Prescott Fire Department.

"Why did you choose to go into that field?" she asked.

"I always admired firefighters," he said. "When I was just a kid I remember firefighters coming to my school and telling us about their jobs. I guess that's when the seed was planted. I went into ranching to start with because that's what my family did. I enjoy it, but it wasn't as fulfilling as serving the community as a firefighter." He thought about those days. "But I love ranching, too, so I have the best of both worlds."

"It sounds like you do," she said softly.

They reached the ranch and rode straight up to the house. He dismounted then helped her get off the horse and left Holly and Molly waiting outside. Carilyn still seemed uninjured with the exception of the concussion and head wound.

Inside he had her lie on the couch. "How's the pain?" he asked.

"I have a dull headache." She pinched the bridge of her nose with her thumb and forefinger. "I think the Tylenol is helping keep a full blown headache away."

"I'll get you some water." He stood and went to the kitchen to get her a glass of ice water and returned a few moments later.

After she'd taken a few sips of the water, he set the glass on the end table. "You rest now. I'm going to check on you every now and then. Okay?"

She let out a sigh. "Right now rest sounds good."

"I'm going to let you sleep for a couple of hours." He gently stroked her hair from her face. "I'll wake you up to check on you then."

"I'm fine." She sighed. "I'll just relax a little."

In a matter of moments she fell asleep, her breathing becoming slow and even.

He watched her until she fell asleep, her features relaxed, the tension in her forehead vanishing. She was beautiful with loose tendrils of her hair around her face, the sprinkling of freckles against her pale skin. She was a little too pale, but she should be fine with some rest.

Tension had formed in his chest the moment she was thrown from the horse, and the tension had stayed. He'd invited her to go riding and she had ended up being in an accident and was now injured. He gritted his teeth. Thank God it hadn't been any worse.

He shook his head. It was possible Carilyn would focus on the negatives of his lifestyle because of the accident. He wouldn't blame her, but he hoped that wouldn't be the case.

With one last look at her, he got up and left her to sleep. He headed outside to take care of Holly and Molly in record time so that he could check on Carilyn again.

When he returned to the house, he looked in on her and she seemed to be sleeping peacefully. He walked away from where she lay and headed through the archway to his office. As he reached his desk, his cell phone rang. He drew it out of the holster on his belt as he settled in his seat.

The caller ID told him it was Reese. "How's it going?" Cody asked as he answered.

"I have an update for you on the arsonist case regarding Janice Barnhart." Reese sounded grim. "We found her vehicle abandoned in the Bradshaw Mountains. There's no trace of her with the exception of her purse, which was left in the car."

Cody frowned and started to pace as he spoke. "Any chance she's just out for a walk?"

"Her car is covered in at least a week's worth of dust and pine needles," Reese said and then added, "We located her parents in Phoenix and they haven't heard from Ms. Barnhart in a week. Her parents said she usually contacts them on Sunday afternoons. They hadn't been too worried because she has missed a Sunday or two in the past."

Reese's mouth tightened as he continued, "Janice told her parents that she would be in town this week working on designing a new dress shop that she plans on opening in the fall. Her parents said she would have told them if she was going out of town."

"Damn." Cody bit out the word as he paced his office. "This doesn't sound good."

"It sure as hell doesn't," Reese said. "I obtained a warrant to search her apartment and the living room was a mess, indicating there could have been a struggle. But it's possible she could just be a messy person. Toiletries were in the bathroom, the clothes closets and drawers were full, there were suitcases in the coat closet, an almost full gallon jug of milk in the fridge, which was filled with groceries, and any number of other clues that tells us she wasn't planning on an extended stay anywhere else."

Cody pushed his hand through his hair in frustration. "What now?"

"We're treating it as a missing person's case and we've started a search," Reese said. "We've started locally and if nothing turns up we'll be searching the area where we found her car."

Cody leaned back in his office chair. "Thanks for keeping me up to speed."

"No problem," Reese said. "I'll be in touch if I have any news."

When he'd disconnected the phone, Cody absently flipped the cell phone in his hands as he thought about what Reese had just told him. Did Janice Barnhart's disappearance have anything to do with the arsonist? Were the other victims of the arsonist in danger, too?

He gritted his teeth. Damned if he was going to let anything happen to Carilyn.

* * * * *

Carilyn's head ached so badly she thought it would split. She gave a low groan as she heard a voice calling to her.

"Wake up, Carilyn." A male voice was speaking her name and a warm hand was on her shoulder. "I need to check on you."

She didn't want to wake up, but she was inclined to obey. She blinked her eyes to a dim room and looked up to see Cody bent over her.

He ran his knuckles along her cheek. "This might seem like a silly question, but what's your name?"

It did seem silly but then she surprised herself when she hesitated. "Carilyn," she said as she pushed through the fog and grasped the answer.

"Do you know where you are?" he asked.

She had to think for a moment. "On your ranch. Outside of Prescott."

He gave a nod. "Do you know what happened to you?"

She frowned. "I…" She had to concentrate hard. Her thoughts seemed so elusive. "There was a rattlesnake and I was thrown from your horse. From Molly. I landed on the ground and hit my head."

"Very good." He raised a cup of water. "I'd bet you'd like some more Tylenol about now."

"You'd bet right." She tried to smile. It hurt.

He helped her sit just enough to swallow the tablets and she chased it down with sips of water. Her mouth and throat were dry and she was glad to have something to drink.

"You can keep on sleeping." He checked her eyes, probably looking to see if they were dilated. Despite her confusion, she seemed to remember that much. "You need to relax and recover. A concussion is nothing to take lightly."

"Okay." She felt too foggy to argue with him. As much as she felt the need to get home and work on her laptop, she also realized the last thing she should be doing now was driving. She wouldn't be able to concentrate on work, anyway.

He put his hand on her shoulder and squeezed as he looked down on her. "Rest," he repeated.

"I will," she said before she drifted off to sleep again.

CHAPTER 9

He hadn't meant to kill her.

Nathan stared at the body of Janice Barnhart, in the abandoned old warehouse, his stomach churning. He had only wanted to scare her.

Right?

But he had pushed too far and everything had gotten out of control.

He tilted his head as he studied Janice where she lay slumped on the concrete floor against the metal support. She looked a lot like the charred blonde Barbie he'd just set fire to in front of Janice while she'd still been alive. He'd tied a gag around the doll, and bound her wrists together and her ankles too, using a chain necklace…just like Janice had been bound with heavy chain.

He hadn't expected Janice's clothes to catch fire.

Or had he known perfectly well what would happen when he tossed the burning doll at Janice's feet?

Her clothes had caught fire so quickly he'd known there was nothing he could do to save her. He'd thrown the blanket he'd covered her with in the car into the fire. The burning blanket had finished the job.

He'd watched her burn. The fire had been amazing, had filled him with an excitement he'd never experienced before.

The gag had muffled her screams and the metal support she was chained to had kept her from moving. The concrete floor in the empty part of the vast warehouse hadn't allowed the fire to spread and it had burned itself out.

The sickly smell and the smoke had him coughing and his eyes stung. Still, he stared at her body, fascinated.

He'd never taken a life before. Instead of sickening him, a sense of power flooded his veins. It was as if her lifeforce had flowed into him and strengthened his own.

Taking her to the warehouse after keeping her in his apartment for a week had been a spur of the moment thing. He'd gotten tired of her constant moaning and hadn't been sure what to do with her once he'd had her.

Rape was distasteful, but even without that he'd felt confident and powerful having her in his possession. He'd been in control of everything she did, day after day.

And now the final testament to his power… Her life had been in his hands… And he'd snuffed it out.

He frowned. What should he do with her body? He looked around the warehouse with all its junk, old and rusted tools, broken down machinery, and refuse. His gaze landed on a group of rusted red and green fifty-gallon drums. One of those would do.

The body was burned beyond recognition, including what had been lovely blonde hair. He didn't want to touch her so he went to his car that was parked nearby in the warehouse, and pulled a tarp out of the trunk.

Once he was back, he crossed the chalk line he'd drawn and poured gasoline on. Carefully, avoiding contact with Janice's charred skin, he unlocked the chains that bound her to the steel support and also removed the chains from around her ankles.

Somehow he managed to roll her body onto the tarp without touching it, and he wrapped her in it. He tied cord around the corpse to keep the tarp from coming off and dragged the body to one of the drums and let the body drop to the floor. It took the crowbar that he took from the back of the car to get the lid off the empty drum.

Nathan wasn't a big man and her dead weight was a challenge to get into the drum. Her tarp-covered body finally slid off his shoulder and fell into the drum with a hard thump. He tossed the remnants of the burned Barbie inside with the body.

With relief, he put the lid back on the drum and used the crow bar to bang the lid down tight. The sound of metal hitting metal echoed in the warehouse.

When he was finished, he tossed the crowbar and the chains into the back of the car. As he made sure he didn't leave anything behind, he worked the scene over and over in his mind.

He thought about how she'd burned…the terror in her eyes… the screams behind her gag…

Unexpectedly, his dinner churned in his belly and started to come up. The next thing he knew, he was puking all over the concrete floor.

Finally, he finished and wiped his mouth with his shirtsleeve as he blinked his watery eyes, and tried to spit the acidic taste out of his mouth. He stared at the mess he'd made then slipped outside into the darkness, scooped up dirt with an old tin can he'd found in the warehouse, and returned to pour the dirt over the vomit. For good measure he found some old crude oil and poured it over the dirt. Puke no doubt would have his DNA, and he didn't want to take any chances.

When he'd finished gathering his supplies, he rolled up the warehouse door and drove his car out. He got out to roll the door back down again and then headed home.

As he drove, the urge to burn again was strong. He should wait. It had just been days ago that he'd torched the redhead's car. And he'd just played with fire once again, for the first time killing his victim.

First things first. He needed to research everything his target did and photograph her.

While he drove from the outskirts of town, his thoughts drifted to the redhead. She had been a spur of the moment decision. He'd needed a redhead and there she was. It had been the perfect opportunity.

Where was she now?

Wherever she was, he would find her.

CHAPTER 10

Every couple of hours, Cody had woken Carilyn to check on her after insisting she lay on his bed, and he'd slept in the guestroom. She'd been so out of it that every time he woke her it had seemed unreal, like a dream.

Now, as she blinked her eyes open, she squinted against the early morning sun coming in through his bedroom window. The clean sheets he'd put on his bed felt wonderful and the T-shirt he had loaned her felt soft against her skin. His scent surrounded her. She liked the way he smelled, a heady masculine scent.

A part of her had wanted to get home at once, and another part knew she had no business driving. Her head was splitting and she still felt foggy, and was having a hard time thinking clearly.

Cody walked into the bedroom, smiling as he saw that she was awake, his brown eyes warm. Despite her headache, she couldn't help but admire the pure masculinity of his presence. He wore a T-shirt that fitted snugly to his muscular frame, stretching around the width of his biceps and across his chest.

He came closer and stood beside the bed, looking down at her. "How are you doing?"

"Hi." She managed a return smile and started to push herself up in bed. Her head swam and she put the heel of her palm to her forehead as if that would stop the spinning. "I guess I've been better."

"You can stay here as long as you need to." The mattress dipped beneath his weight as he sat down on the bed beside her. "There's no rush in leaving."

"You don't need to take care of me." She slid back down again though, fighting a wave of nausea. "Maybe you could give me a ride home to Leigh's and I'll get the car later."

"Not happening." He shook his head. "I'm going to watch you for a full twenty-four hours. After that we'll see how you feel. If Leigh was here to check in on you, that would be one thing. But I'm not leaving you alone."

She sighed. "All right. I hate being any trouble for you."

He rested his hand on her wrist and she looked at it. The hair on his arm was a brownish-gold against his tanned skin. His fingers were long and strong and his touch felt warm and comforting. "You're no trouble."

"Ha," she said, giving him a teasing smile as she met his gaze. "I'm being a big pain."

His expression turned serious. "I'm sorry this happened, honey."

"It wasn't your fault." She put her hand over where his rested on her arm and she liked the feel of his warm skin beneath her palm. "I had a great time." She gave a wry smile. "Up until the rattlesnake spooked Molly. Whatever happened to that snake, anyway?"

His features hardened a little, as if the thought of the snake being a danger to her stirred anger inside him. "That's what the snake shot was for. I buried what was left of the head once I killed it. A rattlesnake's fangs are just as poisonous when it's dead."

"Oh." She let out her breath. "I forgot about the snake shot."

"Are you up to going to the kitchen for breakfast?" he asked. "Or would you like me to serve you in bed?"

Carilyn would have shaken her head if it didn't hurt so much. "I can get up. I need to move around."

He squeezed her arm. "Why don't you swing your legs over the side of the bed and take it easy when you stand. Make sure you're okay to walk."

Her bruised body complained as she sat up in bed and slowly slid her legs off the mattress and stood. His T-shirt fell to midthigh and the tile was cool beneath her bare feet. She felt sore, woozy, and wobbly but she gave him a smile. "I'll be fine. Just give me a chance to put on my jeans."

He left the room and she grimaced as she pulled on her jeans and then she stuffed her phone in her pocket. She headed out of the bedroom with its rustic furniture, and burgundy and forest green curtains and comforter.

"I had no idea that having a concussion could affect me like this," she said as she entered the kitchen and saw Cody.

"Concussions can range from mild to severe, and yours seems to be moderate." He rested his hand on her shoulder when he reached her. "If it gets any worse, we'll get you to a doctor. I know a couple of good ones."

"Thanks." She glanced at him and tried to look like she was smiling and not grimacing. "I'm sure I'm going to be okay."

"I've know people who have seemed all right at the start," he said, "but then it progressed to something much worse. I'll just keep an eye on you."

"Okay." She really couldn't argue with the pounding in her head making it feel like it was splitting.

The kitchen smelled great, of pancakes, bacon, and eggs. She figured her appetite was just fine when her stomach growled.

"Have a seat." He nodded at the kitchen nook table. "I'll bring you a plate."

Ordinarily she would have insisted on helping, but in this case she did as he told her and seated herself at the round oak table. It wasn't long before he was setting in front of her a plate with two four-inch round pancakes, two strips of bacon, and a good-sized portion of scrambled eggs.

"If that's too much, you don't have to eat all of it," he said. "By the same token, if you're still hungry when you finish, there's plenty more."

Carilyn picked up a forkful of eggs and found them to be delicious and her stomach more than happy to receive them. She poured maple syrup on her pancakes. "This is great."

He chewed and swallowed a bite of bacon. "Other than the headache, how are you doing?"

"Sore." She cut into her pancakes with her fork. "But other than that and the headache, I think I'm doing well."

He gave her a look of approval. "Good."

While they ate, he told her a few stories of growing up on the ranch with his brother and parents. It was nice listening to him. He seemed to realize that it hurt her head to talk but she didn't mind hearing him speak.

"Thank you for inviting me and taking care of me." She pushed her plate away. "I like your ranch and I have to say my first visit has been an interesting one."

The corner of his mouth tipped up. "You are one tough lady."

"Why, thank you." She grinned at him. "I'll take that as a compliment."

"It was meant as one." He smiled back at her. He got up and started clearing the breakfast dishes. "Stay there," he said as she started to get up.

She settled back in her seat. "What do you have planned today?"

"I've done the morning chores." He put the dishes in the sink and started rinsing them. "Now I have to finish welding a new feed trough I'm putting together, and later I have some 4-H kids coming over to look at a couple of calves."

"You weld, too?" she said.

He nodded. "You learn a lot of things growing up on a ranch."

"You also like kids," she said. It was clear by the way he smiled when he talked about the 4-H'ers.

"Yep." He grinned. "Hope to have a few of my own running around some day."

"How's a guy like you still single?" Her face warmed as the question came out without her thinking about it. Her head injury must be worse than she thought.

Cody shrugged. "Just haven't found the right woman." He looked at her. "I've been looking, though."

The intensity of his gaze sent a warm rush over her. *Dumb, dumb, dumb to say something like that,* she told herself.

He went on, "I have a couple of exes who live around here." He set the dishtowel he'd been holding onto the countertop. "I try to stay friends, but it doesn't always work out that way."

"I have one of those," she said. "An ex who would never have worked as a friend, but that was a long time ago. Sam, on the other hand, you can't help but like and stay friends with."

"Any chance you and Sam will ever get together again?" Cody asked.

"No." Carilyn shook her head. "Like I told you before, he's a good guy. But as far as us getting together, I've moved on and he's moved on. Friends are all we'll ever be."

Cody slid the last plate into the dishwasher and she was grateful when he changed the subject. "Are you going to be all right while I'm out working?"

She smiled. "Don't worry so much, cowboy. I'll be fine."

"Just want to make sure my patient is okay." He gave her a quick grin. "If you're up to it, you can watch TV in the living room or guestroom. Otherwise, get some rest."

"Now that I'm up and have had breakfast, I'm feeling much better." She pushed hair out of her face. "I think I'd be fine driving home."

He shook his head. "You're staying with me for a full twenty-four hours. If you have to go home, then I'm going with you and you aren't driving. Got that?"

She raised her hands. "Okay, okay. I'll be good."

"I'm glad to hear that." He gave her a quick grin. "Now behave yourself."

"Would you have a computer I can borrow to check my email and surf the net?" she asked.

"You can use mine." He gave a nod in the direction of the hallway. "It's in my office."

She followed him to a room with a large rustic-style desk along with a wood file cabinet and piles of papers on the file cabinet and on the desktop. He went the laptop desk and keyed in the password.

He moved away from the office chair. "Have a seat."

"Thank you." She smiled at him, not ready to tell him she could likely hack into his computer with minimal trouble with her skillset.

She eased into the chair and scooted it up to the computer. His wallpaper was a picture of the ranch taken after a rain, with water glistening on blades of grass and the sky reflected in the water puddles on the ground. "It looks like a professional photographer took the picture you're using for your wallpaper," she said to Cody.

"An old friend stopped by the ranch and took it," Cody said. "She's an amateur, but her work looks professional."

Carilyn nodded. "It sure does."

"You probably aren't going to feel like spending a lot of time on the computer," he said. "But regardless, take a break after an hour at most."

"Okay, doc." She smiled. "I'll lie down if I start to feel bad and I'll take that mandatory break when it's time."

"Good girl." He rested his hand on her shoulder and squeezed. "Do you have your cell phone?"

She dug it out of her pocket and held it up. He took it from her and pressed a few buttons. "I'm putting my number in your contacts." When he finished, he handed the iPhone back to her. She took it and saw "Cody McBride" listed in her contacts along with a phone number beneath it. "Call me if you need *anything*." He stressed the last word.

"I will." She held up her fingers and crossed them. "Promise."

He surprised her by bending over and kissing her on top of the head and then drew away. "I'll be back in a bit."

She smiled at him as he looked at her one more time then turned and walked out of the office. She stared after him, enjoying the backside view like she had done the first time she'd ever seen him. Damn, he was hot.

Rolling her eyes up to the ceiling she mentally shook her head. This was ridiculous. She sighed and looked at the beautiful photo wallpaper of the ranch. It was a beautiful place.

She pulled up the Internet browser, went to her email client, and logged in. She wasn't surprised when she saw a hoard of emails and she groaned. Trying to focus on the screen while she had a concussion was bad enough. Maybe she'd just come back to it later.

Just as she was about to close out the browser, the title of an email caught her attention. She frowned as she looked at it. The sender was "Firebug" and the subject line was "Redhead."

She moved the cursor and clicked to open the email. Her blood went cold and chilled her veins when she saw the four words in the body of the email.

You're next, Carilyn Thompson.

CHAPTER 11

Carilyn chewed her thumbnail as she stared at the email. She hadn't chewed her nails since she had suffered from a panic disorder all those years ago, but the email had brought on the sudden burst of anxiety.

You're next, Carilyn Thompson.

What did it mean? Who was "Firebug"? Was he the person who had torched her car? How did he know her name? How had he found her?

The questions blew through her mind, making her head ache even more. She took deep breaths and slowly blew out through her mouth, trying to calm the jittery feeling that was taking over her body.

Okay. She wasn't a hacker for nothing. She could trace this sonofabitch down. All she had to do was calm herself, put on her analytical cap, and find him.

The IP address led her nowhere and she didn't have the software she needed to take her very far. Still, she did everything she could. The person who'd sent her that email was good at hiding his tracks from what she could tell. She was going to have to get on her own laptop, install software, and dig deeper.

When she'd gone as far as she could go, she leaned back in the office chair. Her head was splitting and she was having a difficult time focusing. It hadn't helped her search not being able to think clearly thanks to the concussion.

Being busy trying to track "Firebug" down had kept the anxiety at bay. But as she sat in the chair staring at the email again, panic started to claw its way up her throat. She closed her eyes and clenched her fists on the desktop. She was not going to let this person destroy the years of hard work it had taken to get to where she was now.

Again she took deep breaths and let them out slowly. She worked to focus outward and not on the way her skin was crawling and the tight ball forming in her chest. She swallowed and unclenched her fists before clenching them again.

Her headache and mental confusion from the concussion was making it harder to concentrate on relaxing. But she shoved her way through it, determined not to let this get the best of her and destroy her hard-won control.

She pushed back the chair, but stood too fast. Her head swam and she had to brace her hands on the desktop to steady herself. When she felt like she could walk, she raised her head and walked toward the office door.

The front door closed hard and she jumped. Her heart thudded, as if it might be the mysterious e-mailer who was coming in the front door of Cody's house. Which was completely crazy. The person would have no idea she was here.

But he'd known her name. Her full name. And he'd found her email address.

Rational thought clashed with irrational ones.

What if Firebug knows where I am now? What if that's him?

No, that was impossible. No one but Cody knew where she was.

What if Firebug has been following me?

She would have noticed anything suspicious.

Would I really have noticed?

The back and forth in her mind was about to drive her crazy and it was only ratcheting up the anxiety that was making her chest hurt.

She heard the sound of heavy shoes on tile. It sounded like boots. Without really processing what she was doing, she picked up a heavy glass paperweight with a scorpion trapped in the glass and held the paperweight in her fist. She backed up against the wall beside the door and raised her arm. She held her breath.

Another footstep. Closer.

At the door.

"Carilyn?" Cody called out.

Air rushed from Carilyn's chest and she sagged against the wall as Cody stepped into the room.

He frowned. "Are you all right?"

She managed a nod.

"You look upset." He was still frowning.

"I'm okay." She tried for a smile.

He nodded toward her hand. "Planning on playing a little baseball?"

She glanced at the paperweight she was holding and immediately felt silly. She put the object on the desktop. "I just got a little spooked."

Now Cody's expression turned to concerned. "What happened?"

"I received a strange email." She gestured to his laptop. The email was still open.

"Do you mind if I read it?" he asked.

She shook her head.

He eased down into the chair and looked at the email. Immediately his expression went hard.

He looked over his shoulder at her. "I assume you don't know this 'Firebug.'"

She shook her head. "I have no idea who could have sent it." She took a deep breath. "I have some talent at tracking people down myself and the IP address took me nowhere and I don't have the software I need to take it any further."

Cody nodded slowly. "I need to show this to Reese."

"Your cousin, the detective?" Carilyn asked.

"Yes." Cody clicked the button to print and the printer started humming. "It's only a theory, but I'm afraid this might be related to the arsonist." He looked at her. "You are not going anywhere without me."

She dragged her hand down her braid and started plucking the end, another one of her high anxiety habits. She was aware of it, but she couldn't get herself to stop doing it. "I can't just hide."

Cody got up from his seat and took her by the shoulders. "More importantly, you can't take chances. Until this guy is caught, you need to stay low."

"What if it's an idle threat?" She frowned. "What if someone is trying to scare me as a prank?"

Cody didn't release his light grip on her. "One of the other arsonist's victims is missing. Police don't know if it's related, but this email concerns me."

A cold chill prickled Carilyn's skin. "Missing?"

"It may be nothing." Cody caressed her upper arms soothingly. "But the police are treating it as a missing person's case."

The thought that everything could be tied to the arsonist made her stomach clench. "What do I do?"

"You continue to hang out with me." He smiled at her. "Is that such a bad thing?"

She couldn't help a little smile. "These are great lengths to go to in order to keep me around."

He smiled in return, but it was a concerned smile. "Are you okay?"

She nodded. "I'm fine. But I need my laptop and software so that I can work to track down the S.O.B. who sent the email. I also need to get clothes and toiletries."

"I'll take you to Leigh's to get some of your things." Cody slid his hands down her arms and released her. "We'll go while it's still broad daylight. Are you up to going now?"

"Now is good." She followed him out the office door. "I'll get my purse." She glanced down at his T-shirt that she was wearing. "And I'll put on my own clothes."

"I'll be in the kitchen," he said.

She hurried down the hall and found that Cody had washed her clothes while she slept and had stacked them in a neat pile on the trunk at the foot of the bed. She pulled on her T-shirt, jeans, socks, and shoes, taking her time because she still wasn't steady on her feet. When she was finished, she grabbed her purse and headed back toward the kitchen.

Cody was leaning up against the counter with a glass of milk in one hand and an Oreo cookie in the other. He nodded toward the open package on the counter. "Cookie?"

"I'm still full from breakfast." She cocked her head to the side. "Isn't it a little early to be eating cookies?"

Cody gave her a quick grin. "It's never too early for Oreos." He glanced at the clock. "Besides, it's closing in on eleven."

"Wow." She looked from the clock to him. "I had no idea that much time had passed since breakfast."

"We can hit the drive-thru on the way back from Leigh's place." He put his empty milk glass in the dishwasher. "There's a great burger joint in town."

After Cody put away the Oreos, he and Carilyn left the house and climbed into his truck. She kept a tight grip on her purse, as if that could protect her like some kind of shield. Protect her from what, she wasn't sure, but holding it to her chest was somehow comforting.

"While you were getting dressed, I called Reese." Cody glanced from the road to Carilyn. "He said he was concerned about your safety based on the letter and additional circumstances." Cody glanced back at the road. "He obtained a warrant to search the first victim's home, and it looked like there could have been a fight inside, but it's not conclusive."

Carilyn sucked in her breath. "Do they think it's the same person who sent me the email?"

Cody's expression grew grimmer. "They've sent her computer to forensics but they did get a response back right away to let Reese know they found an email from someone who called himself Firebug." Cody continued as hair rose on Carilyn's arms, "His message was a little different, but Reese thinks it might be the same guy."

Carilyn swallowed. "What did it say?"

"The email read, 'I'm watching you,'" Cody said. "And he used her name, too."

Shaking her head, Carilyn rubbed her arms with her palms. "This is crazy. I just got into town. I haven't had time to make any enemies."

"I believe you may just have been in the wrong place at the wrong time." Cody's knuckles whitened as he gripped the steering wheel. "There are things I can't tell you about—not yet—that lead both Reese and me to that conclusion."

"You asked me about having a doll with me in my car and I told you no," Carilyn said. "Does it have anything to do with that?"

"I'll tell you when I can," Cody said and she knew he wasn't going to explain what was going on any more than that.

When they reached Leigh's home, Carilyn was surprised to see a police cruiser and a sedan pulled up in front of the house. Detective Reese McBride and a police officer in uniform were standing on the porch.

She looked at Cody. "What are the police doing here?"

"Insurance," Cody said as he parked the truck. "Just making sure it's safe to go in."

Cody jumped out of the truck, came around to the passenger side, and opened the door. He took Carilyn's hand. "Easy does it," he said.

"Thanks." Her head was feeling a little better, but still woozy and she was a little unsteady on her feet.

Detective McBride walked toward them. "How are you feeling, Ms. Thompson?" he asked. "Cody tells me you took a spill from a horse."

"Could be better," she said, "but I'm doing fine."

"Do you have the key?" the detective asked.

She handed over the key and stood on the sidewalk beside the truck as he and the police officer checked the house.

When they came out, Detective McBride was frowning. "I need you to take a look at the house."

Carilyn's heart beat a little faster as they walked up the stairs. "What's wrong?"

He gestured to the front door. "Tell me if the house is in the same condition you left it in."

"All right." Not knowing what to expect, Carilyn stepped into the house. The hair on her arms rose.

It was a disaster with a vase shattered on the floor, a lamp that had been knocked over and broken, couch cushions in disarray, and a plant on its side and dirt spilled across the floor.

"No." She looked at the detective, the words barely coming out of her mouth. "It was clean and orderly when I left."

"Why don't you see if you notice anything missing," Detective McBride said.

"I don't know that much about Leigh's things." Carilyn picked her way through the mess. "So far I can't tell." She knelt when she saw the framed photograph of Leigh, Misha, and herself, and picked it up off the floor. The glass was shattered. She shook her head and placed the photo on an end table.

She made it to the guest bedroom, which had been tossed, too. Her gaze fell on the place where the box for her new computer had been and her stomach bottomed out. It was gone.

"My new computer is missing." She looked over her shoulder at the detective and Cody who were watching. She went to her suitcase. Everything had been thrown out and the software that had been shipped to her was gone. She told the detective. "That software can't be used by anyone without an encrypted passcode, so it's not likely he can break into it."

But that would mean she'd have to have more software shipped to her and purchase another laptop. She put her hand to her forehead, trying to hold back tears.

Cody was at her side in a moment, his arm around her shoulders. "Are you okay?"

She held back a rush of emotion that made the back of her eyes ache and her headache worsen. "I'm okay." Her voice cracked a little. "It's just such a violation."

"Yes, it is." Cody squeezed her shoulders. "Let's get you out of here."

"I need to change first and gather a few things." She looked at her clothing, which had been thrown all over the room. "It might take me a few minutes."

"Take your time," Cody said and he and the detective walked out of the bedroom and closed the door behind them.

A tear trickled from her eye and she brushed it away with the back of her hand. Crying wasn't going to do a damn bit of good.

No, she had to get a computer and had to set it up. She was going to find the bastard. And she was going to find him soon.

* * * * *

Cody wanted Carilyn to go back to the ranch and rest, but she convinced him that she needed to pick up another laptop first. She knew what she wanted and needed, so it was just a matter of getting a second one.

She also made a phone call to a co-worker who said he'd get software she needed to do her job overnighted to her again so that she could get it installed ASAP. He was a hacker, too and was also sending her tracer software on the side.

When they reached the ranch Carilyn did listen to Cody and laid down on the bed in the guestroom and took a nap. She woke in the early evening and found that she was feeling better. Her head hurt less and even though she felt bruised and battered from the spill she'd taken, she felt stronger.

Still, the e-mailer who called himself Firebug had her feeling uneasy and jumpy. The man, at least she assumed it was a man, had not only sent her a threatening email, but had probably been the one to tear apart Leigh's house. The thought of that violation caused anger to burn beneath her skin.

After she had brushed her hair and washed her face, she headed into the kitchen. A note that Cody had written was on the kitchen island, telling her he was outside taking care of chores and would be back shortly.

Her stomach growled. It had been awhile since they'd eaten at a fast food place while they'd gone shopping. She didn't consider herself to be much of a cook, but she figured there had to be something to throw together that would be easy and palatable.

She searched through the pantry and saw that he had a couple of boxes of spaghetti and a jar of red sauce. In the freezer she found frozen vegetables—a man after her own heart. Whenever she bought fresh vegetables they inevitably went bad because of how little she cooked. She located hamburger in the freezer, too. She also found a bag of salad, along with a bottle of Thousand Island dressing as well as a bottle of ranch.

It wasn't long before she'd made meatballs. The spaghetti sauce bubbled in a small pot on the stove, and she added the baked meatballs to it when it was time. She then put the dry spaghetti into water she had boiling in a stockpot she'd found in one of the cabinets. Veggies simmered on a back burner and the salad was in a large bowl on the counter.

"Something smells good." Cody's deep voice had Carilyn whirling around to face him.

"Spaghetti and meatballs," she said. "I assume you like spaghetti since it was in the pantry."

The corner of his mouth curved up in a smile. "You assume right." His expression turned concerned. "How are you feeling?"

"Much, much better." She picked up a pair of potholders she'd discovered in a drawer. She started to put them on to lift the pot and pour the spaghetti into the colander she'd set in the sink.

"Let me." He took the potholders from her, put them on, carried the stockpot to the sink, and poured the spaghetti into the colander. "I don't think you should be carrying anything this heavy."

She shook her head. "I think you're worrying too much about me."

"I'm entitled." He set the empty stockpot on a trivet then shook the colander to get most of the water out. "I watched you take a hell of a spill."

"Well, I'm doing lots better." She turned off the burners that were beneath the veggies and sauce.

In a matter of moments, they had everything on the table and were seated. Dinner was enjoyable and she was glad he didn't bring up "Firebug" or anything else that had happened. When they'd finished dinner, they cleaned up. He said he'd offer her a glass of wine but that she should stay away from alcohol until she was fully healed from the concussion or it could delay her healing.

Carilyn was surprised at how easily she had settled in to staying with Cody despite the fact that they'd only met a few days ago. She found she trusted him and was comfortable with him.

After dinner, she asked Cody to play his guitar. He got it out and sang as he played a few tunes for her. He had a great singing voice and she loved listening to him. As far as she was concerned, he finished too soon—she could listen to him all night long and not get tired of it.

Once he'd put away his guitar, he suggested watching a pay-per-view movie on cable. They picked out the latest superhero movie when they discovered they each liked Spiderman, Superman, Batman, Ironman, and any other number of superhero movies. When she sat on the couch, he sat on it too, close but not so close that she might feel he was going to try to be intimate. She wasn't ready for that. She still had a headache, not to mention she didn't plan on getting involved with him since she was here for such a short amount of time.

The movie was fun but at the end she found herself sleepy. "Ready for bed?" he asked when she yawned.

"Sorry." She held back another yawn. "I think the day is getting to me."

He shifted on the couch. "Do you have everything you need in the guestroom?"

She nodded. "Now that I have my clothes and toiletries, I'm all set. Tomorrow I should be okay to go back to Leigh's."

His forehead wrinkled as he frowned. "I don't like the idea of you going back to Leigh's after the place was just ransacked, and when you're getting threatening emails."

"Maybe I'll book a room in a hotel." She sighed. "I can't just stay here with you. I think I'm wearing out my welcome."

He reached out and put his hand over hers. His touch was warm, comforting. "Carilyn, you are welcome here as long as you need. I'd rather see you here where I can keep an eye on you. I have to admit I'd be damned worried if you were out there alone."

She smiled and surprised herself as she turned her hand up and clasped his. "Don't worry so much."

"Can't help it." He studied her for a long moment, looking as though he wanted to say something. Instead he leaned closer and her belly flipped as she thought he was going to kiss her, but he pressed his lips to her forehead then drew back. "Now let's get you to bed."

CHAPTER 12

Early the next morning, Monday, Cody headed outside to take care of chores. He frowned as he thought about the person who called himself Firebug, the threatening email to Carilyn, and someone trashing Leigh's house.

Dawn was just lifting the dark sky, graying it out, the sun starting to peek over the horizon. It promised to be a beautiful day, yet what had happened yesterday cast a shadow over everything.

He fed the cattle and horses, checked the water troughs, saw to the trees being irrigated around the ranch, and generally made sure everything was running smoothly. When he headed back into the house, the smell of coffee and sausages filled the air and he heard the meat sizzling on the stovetop.

When he went to the entryway to the kitchen, he leaned against the doorframe, watching Carilyn as she busied herself. She hadn't noticed him and he smiled to himself as he thought about what it would be like to come in every day to find her cooking breakfast for them. She looked cute in her jeans and T-shirt, her feet bare, and her damp red hair pulled back in a ponytail. From her wet hair, he guessed she'd just taken a shower.

She glanced over her shoulder and smiled. "Good morning."

"Good morning to you, sunshine." He pushed away from the doorframe and walked closer to her. "Smells great."

"Coffee is ready." She nodded toward the coffee maker. "I'm just about to make omelets. Two eggs or three, and what do you like on yours?"

He looked over the plate of grated cheddar cheese, chopped onions, fresh tomatoes cut into small pieces, and bell pepper sliced into small pieces, too. "Three eggs and I'll take everything on it," he said.

"You've got it." She beat eggs in a bowl with a whisk. "They won't be pretty but they'll be edible."

He laughed. "Edible is what counts." He studied her as she poured the egg into the nonstick pan. "How are you feeling?"

"Better." She glanced at him. "Still have a headache and sometimes I'm a little unsteady on my feet, but I think I'll be fine to go back to Leigh's later today or tomorrow."

"Don't rush it, Carilyn," he said as she put cheese and veggies in the omelet. "There's no hurry to leave and it may not be safe to go to Leigh's."

She looked up from the omelet. "I don't want to be a burden."

He tweaked her ponytail and caught a whiff of the soap she'd used when she'd taken a shower. "And I told you that you are not a burden." He gave her a little grin. "Besides, what cowboy doesn't want to come in to a warm breakfast rather than eating cold cereal on his own?"

"There is that," she said with a smile.

While she made breakfast, he made himself a cup of coffee, black. He set the table for two, including glasses and a jug of orange juice. He also took a jar of salsa out of the fridge along with a tub of sour cream, something he liked on his omelets. When she was finished, she was right, they weren't pretty, but they smelled great and tasted even better.

Over breakfast they talked about her plans for the day. "I need to start setting up my laptop as much as I can without the software," she said. "There are some things I can download off the Internet."

"I don't think I'd be much of a help there," he said as he cut into his omelet with his fork. "I'm doing good to utilize whatever software I need for work at the fire department or here for the ranch." He ate the bite of omelet. After he swallowed, he said, "So you know how to track people down on the Internet?"

She nodded. "Even people who try to cover up their tracks. Eventually I will find them."

"You must be good at what you do," Cody said.

With a shrug she said, "It's what I was trained to do and something I have a knack at doing."

"How did you get in that line of work?" he asked.

"I majored in computer science when I was in college." She smiled, finally deciding to tell him what she actually did. "I did post-graduate work in programming and I got involved with an elite group of programmers—hackers—who taught me a whole lot about what I do now. You could say I have a gift for it."

Cody raised his brows. "You're a hacker?"

She gave an impish grin. "For the good guys."

"That's pretty cool." Cody took a drink of juice and set the glass down, thumping it on the tabletop. "So you think you can find Firebug?"

"Eventually." Her brow wrinkled. "Firebug did a credible job covering his tracks, but I'll be getting software that will help me get to him."

Cody gave a satisfied nod. "As soon as we find him, I'm going after the bastard."

Carilyn was taken aback and her eyes widened. "You're not going after Firebug on your own, are you?"

Cody looked like he was considering it. "I'll call Reese," Cody finally said. "He'll likely let me in on the action—or at least watch it." His gaze met Carilyn's. "But if the bastard tries to hurt you all bets are off."

Again, he looked as if he wanted to say more, but didn't. Some kind of connection was between them and she knew he felt it too.

After breakfast, they cleaned up together. When they were finished, he put his arm around her shoulders and gave her a little squeeze. "This afternoon, I have a few 4-H'ers coming over to look at my calves. You're welcome to join us and meet the kids."

"I might do that." She smiled at him.

"Come on out if you decide you want to." He released her, headed to the front door, and took a beat-up work-worn western hat off of the hat rack. He tugged the hat down on his forehead and opened the door.

Carilyn watched Cody walk out of the house. She never got tired of seeing his sexy backside. She also liked the feeling of being in the same house as him, making him breakfast as he came in from work. It was a homey, comfortable feeling.

She shook her head. This was exactly why it wasn't a good idea to stay at the ranch with Cody. Jeez, soon she'd be heading back to Kansas and she could end up hurting both of them if she wasn't careful.

It took some time to install the basic software on her new laptop, just to get it up and running. It was frustrating not having the software to prepare to tackle her job, but she'd just have to make up for lost time by working longer hours after she received the software.

She downloaded tracing software that a fellow hacker provided when she contacted him. Or her—it was virtually impossible to tell from their names. This hacker was referred to as Lord. His/her whole name was LordoftheFuneralPyre. It sounded masculine to her, but who really knew? Carilyn went by WizardAsp as her hacker name, which she figured was as androgynous as one could get.

When she was finished setting up her laptop the way she wanted it, she decided to head to the kitchen. She poked around until she found an old recipe book with one page marked. It was a recipe for chewy brownies. Despite the fact that she wasn't the best cook, she did know how to make brownies. As long as she didn't burn them, they should turn out fine.

First she checked to make sure Cody had all the ingredients to make the brownies and was pleased when she found everything. He was almost out of cocoa and flour, but there was enough to get by. It didn't take long until she had all of the ingredients combined and was stirring the batter. She greased a pan and spread the mixture into it before putting it into a preheated oven.

While the brownies baked, she brought her laptop into the kitchen and checked her email again, praying she didn't have one from Firebug. Thankfully she didn't.

Just as she was going to close out the email client, a new one popped into her inbox. *Sam Anthony.*

"Sam?" she said as she straightened in her chair. She hadn't heard from him since he'd gone into the Peace Corps.

She clicked on the email and read it through.

> *Hi, Carilyn,*
> *I just got back to the States yesterday and I wanted to talk with you. I went to your apartment earlier today but you weren't there, and you didn't answer your phone when I called.*

Carilyn paused to pull her phone out of her pocket and saw that yes, she'd missed two calls from him. She frowned but then saw that somehow her ringer had been turned off. She went back to reading the email.

> *I wanted to tell you how much I've missed you and that I'm back for good. Call me. I want to see you.*
> *Love,*
> *Sam*

Carilyn blinked. Sam was back and he wanted to see her? She bit her lower lip. In the past she might have been excited to receive an email from him...but now?

She wondered, too, about him being back for good. Didn't they have to sign a contract or something, like they did in the army? He hadn't explained when he told her and she'd been in too much shock to think to ask.

The smell of something burning caught her attention. "Nooo," she said as she jumped up from her seat, grabbed a couple of potholders, and opened the oven door. She groaned when she saw that the brownies were very dark and very overdone.

"Darn it." She scowled. "These will be extra chewy if they're not as hard as bricks."

She put the pan on a trivet to cool and went back to her laptop. She wasn't ready to respond to Sam, so she closed the laptop lid and wandered to the front door.

She knew what she'd do. She'd try not to think about Sam, the Firebug, or the burnt brownies and go outside for some fresh air and to see what Cody was up to. When she stepped out of the house, she saw him with a group of three kids and three horses stood behind them. From a distance she couldn't tell how old the kids were.

With her hands in the back pockets of her jeans, she strolled toward Cody and the kids. The four of them were outside a corral with five calves in it.

"These heifers are the best of the herd," Cody was saying. "All come from champion stock."

Carilyn watched as the two girls and one boy, all of about eleven or twelve, talked with Cody. They discussed growth rate, reproductive efficiency, conformation, skeletal correctness, and disposition. She liked watching the way he interacted with the kids, on their level. He didn't talk down to them. He engaged the 4-H'ers as adults, answering all of their questions and comments.

Cody surprised Carilyn by drawing her into the group and introducing her to the kids. "Everyone, this is Carilyn," he said. Then he gestured to each kid as he continued. "Carilyn, meet Amanda, Cindy, and Garth Johnson."

"I take it you're all related." She smiled and shook each of their hands as they told her they were cousins. "Have you picked out which calves you want?" she asked.

"This is my first time," Cindy said. She gestured to a heifer, the largest of the bunch. "She's pretty and I like her disposition."

"Not me." Amanda shook her head and pointed to the one closest to them. "I think she has the best lines and show quality."

The boy picked his out of the remaining three heifers and seemed satisfied with his choice. They discussed price and Cody looked like he was holding back amusement and approval at their attempts at haggling.

"You all drive a hard bargain." He looked at each one of them. "I'm going to give you an excellent price, and it is the lowest I will go."

When he gave them the price the kids chimed in their agreement. He promised to keep the heifers for them until they each returned later that evening with their parents. Looking thoroughly excited, the 4-H'ers each mounted a horse and then took off at a fast trot.

"You're good with children," Carilyn said as they headed toward the ranch house.

"I like kids." Cody smiled. "Want a few of my own one day."

Carilyn smiled, too. "So do I."

As they walked, Cody put his arm around her shoulders. It felt comfortable and natural, and she didn't shy away.

When they reached the house and walked inside, Cody sniffed the air. "Do I smell brownies?"

She gave a little laugh. "Burnt brownies."

He looked at her and grinned. "My favorite."

"Uh-huh," she said and shook her head, but he grinned.

They walked inside and went into the kitchen. They sat at the table, drank cold milk, and ate the burnt brownies. She was surprised that he ate half the pan along with two tall glasses of milk. She ate three brownies herself. They weren't too bad for being burnt.

"My mom used to make these." He brushed crumbs off his fingers and onto the plate. "Outside of Oreo cookies, they're my favorite."

"Sorry to ruin them for you," Carilyn said.

He reached out and touched the side of her face. "That was my mom's recipe and what you made is great. Thank you for making the brownies for me."

She couldn't help smiling in return. He was so genuine and sincere. "You're welcome," she said.

He let his hand drop away from her face, but his gaze remained on her. "You manage to surprise me," he said.

She raised her brows. "I hope that's not a bad thing."

"No, it's not a bad thing at all." The corner of his mouth curved. "You're a beautiful women who happens to be a computer geek; you bounced back from a head injury sooner than I expected; you're brave; you're genuine; and you even made me brownies."

She laughed. "Burnt brownies."

"Best burnt brownies I ever ate," he said with a grin then leaned forward and brushed his lips over hers.

CHAPTER 13

Carilyn sat on the porch swing, alone for a second day. Cody had taken four days off from work, which apparently wasn't usual—he had traded with another firefighter so that he could stay with Carilyn an extra day. Starting Monday it had been time for him to work a forty-eight hour shift where he would sleep at the fire department and then he'd have seventy-two hours off.

The butterfly soft feeling of his lips against hers had left her tingling. All he'd done was give her that light kiss and it had made her body warm and desire him in a way she'd never expected. She wondered what would have happened the next day if he hadn't had to leave for his shift at the fire department. Would he have kissed her again? Would it have become more than a kiss?

If anything, she had to count herself lucky. If he'd been around these past days, she might have done something she would have regretted.

She had argued with Cody about going back to Leigh's, but in the end she'd agreed to stay put at his house for safety's sake. However, she'd insisted that when he was back that she was going to go to Leigh's to clean up the mess that had been made when it was ransacked.

The metal pole on the porch swing was cool beneath her palm as she gripped it while she pushed the swing to and fro with one foot. She was waiting for the mail carrier to show up to deliver the package that contained what she needed to get to work. Cody had said the mail carrier, Gisele, arrived between 10:15 and 10:30 like clockwork, unless it was rainy or stormy. Today was another clear day, so she figured there shouldn't be a problem in the mail carrier arriving on time.

Tom, the retired rancher who worked for Cody, was out in the barn cleaning the stalls. From what Cody said, the rancher didn't mind the dirty work that he did to supplement his retirement. Cody had felt more comfortable about leaving Carilyn at the house because Tom was there, and the older man kept a pistol in a holster hanging from his belt. He had a weapons permit and always "packed heat" as he referred to it. Tom was a nice man and she liked him, and it did make her feel better to know he was armed.

Dirt boiled up from the road in the distance and Carilyn watched to see if it was the mail truck. When it came closer, she saw that it was and she waited for the truck to cross the cattle guard, travel down the long driveway, and pull up in front of the house.

She rubbed her palms on her jeans, got up from her seat, and met the postal carrier as she got out of the truck.

"Are you Carilyn Thompson?" The woman with graying hair asked as she came toward Carilyn.

"Yes." Carilyn smiled and took the clipboard from the carrier. "You must be Gisele."

Gisele nodded. "That's me."

"Nice to meet you." Carilyn signed, and then gave the clipboard back to Gisele.

"Have a good day." The carrier gave Carilyn the small box, turned away, and went back to the postal truck before driving off.

After Gisele left, Carilyn headed into the house. It was cool inside but bright because the shades were open. She went to Cody's office where she'd been setting up her laptop and she settled into the office chair. It took some time to load all of the software.

When she was finished loading software, she went to the kitchen and fixed herself a peanut butter and jelly sandwich along with a tall glass of milk. She took it to the office and ate while she finished organizing the computer's desktop just the way she liked it.

"Phew." She leaned back in the chair when she was finished. The PB&J sandwich and glass of milk were gone and she toyed with the idea of another sandwich but decided to stay where she was and work instead considering she was a few days behind now. She'd have to wait to track down Firebug, too, because she needed to do her job. When she was ready she'd set up a tracer program.

Soon she was lost in her work. She enjoyed contracting for the government, which was much better than actually being in a permanent position with Uncle Sam. She had freedom in the number of hours she worked, the days she worked, and the ability to do whatever it took to get the job done. It would come in handy some day when she stayed home to raise a family.

That thought made her think of Cody and what it would be like to have a family with him.

She groaned, shook her head, and got back to work.

When she finished, she felt tired and realized she'd overdone it. She'd been working for hours with only a long enough break to fix herself lunch. She'd been feeling a lot better overall, but she hadn't fully recovered from the concussion. Now she was exhausted and her head ached.

She always kept her email closed when she worked so that she wouldn't be distracted by anything that came in. She'd also been worried that she'd receive something else from Firebug. When she opened it she saw a couple of emails from friends, several work-related emails, and a message from Sam. Thank God there wasn't one from Firebug. She even checked her spam folders, just to make sure.

Her gaze lingered on the new one from Sam. She had meant to respond to him when she'd received the first one, but had forgotten to. He was probably concerned about her because she'd always been good about replying to him, even after they had broken up.

She clicked on the email to open and read it.

> *Carilyn,*
> *Are you off on one of your jaunts*
> *in some exotic locale with Leigh?*
> *Where? When do you return*
> *home? I need to see you.*
> *Love,*
> *Sam*

Carilyn worried her lower lip as she reread his email. He had signed both emails with "love Sam" and she wasn't sure how to take that. Surely he didn't want to get back together with her?

She leaned back in the chair and stared at the computer screen. She had no intention of getting back with Sam again, if that was what he wanted to talk about. But then again, she might just be jumping to conclusions. For all she knew, he had met someone and was inviting Carilyn to the wedding.

Did that thought bother her? She tilted her head to the side as she considered it. Yeah, she had to admit it would be difficult seeing Sam in love with another woman. At the same time, Carilyn also realized that she had moved on. It might be hard to see him marry another woman, but she could accept it.

For now she'd take it as he probably meant it—just a friendly note that he was thinking about her. She might as well let him know that it would be a month before she got back to Kansas City.

She didn't plan on telling him about her car or Firebug—not now. She wanted this whole thing to be done and over with and didn't want him to be worried about her while she was gone.

> *Sam,*
>
> *It was a nice surprise to hear from you and I hope you are doing well. I'm staying in Prescott, AZ to watch Leigh's house while she's in Europe. I'll call you when I get back in town sometime during the middle of next month, and we can catch up then.*
>
> *Take care,*
>
> *Carilyn*

After she pressed send, she shut the lid on her computer. She found herself wishing that Cody was here, but he wouldn't return until tomorrow morning when he got off of his shift. He had called her last night, checking on her, but hadn't been able to talk for long.

As she wandered toward the kitchen, her cell phone rang. She drew it out and saw that it was Cody. Her heart skipped a beat and she smiled as she answered it. "Hi, Cody."

"Hey there, sunshine." A smile was in his voice. "How was your day?"

"Tiring, but good." She gripped the phone as she walked toward the living room, a smile on her own face. "My software came in today and I'm all set up."

"That's great." He hesitated. "No unwanted emails?"

"None." She shook her head. "Just the usual related to business and a couple of emails from friends." She wasn't going to bring up Sam in particular. "How was your day?"

"A second grade class from the elementary school came to the station for a field trip." He said it with enthusiasm. "Love how the kids' eyes light up when they see the fire truck and ask questions."

After seeing him with the 4-H'ers, Carilyn would bet anything that he'd made the field trip fun for the kids. He'd make a great father, too. She could just tell from being around him and the way he talked about kids.

She sat on the couch and curled her legs under her as she held the phone to her ear. "Having a group of kids come to the fire department sounds like fun."

"It was." He paused. "Now be truthful. How are you feeling? Headaches, nausea, coordination?"

"I'm feeling a lot better and much steadier on my feet." She shifted on the couch. "Give me another day and I'm sure I'll be good as new and ready to go back to Leigh's."

"I'll be the judge of that." He sounded both amused and serious at the same time. "I don't want you overdoing it."

"I won't." She crossed her fingers like a little kid. "You worry too much, cowboy."

"Never," he said. "You'll be all right there tonight?"

"Yes, yes, yes," she said with pretend exasperation. "I'm perfectly fine, Mr. McBride."

"Call me if you need anything," he said. "I mean *anything*."

In a serious voice she said, "I'd like some bonbons and a satin pillow. Oh, and bring me a feathered boa and a diamond tiara while you're at it."

"Anything for you, princess." He laughed. "But for now I have to get back to work."

"See you in the morning," she said.

"See you."

When she disconnected the call, she let out a little sigh. She liked talking with Cody. It was comfortable and natural, as if they'd been friends for years. How had she so easily fallen into this comfortable rapport with him?

Yes, it was very comfortable...perhaps too much so?

* * * * *

Cody had found himself driving home faster than he should have, all because he couldn't get his mind off of Carilyn. He was on the last stretch of highway before home as a pair of flashing blue and red lights appeared in his rearview mirror. He groaned. Even with cousins on the police force, that didn't make him immune from getting a ticket.

He sighed and pulled the truck over onto the side of the road. He buzzed down the window as he waited with his hands on the wheel for the officer to come to the window.

"So, where's the fire?" came a familiar deep voice.

Cody looked up to see his cousin, John McBride's, not so amused expression. Reflective sunglasses hid John's eyes, and Cody couldn't tell if his older cousin was serious or not.

"Hi, cuz." Cody let out his breath, hopeful that John wasn't going to give him a ticket.

John was a big man, a hard man, and he had his clipboard in hand. "Cody, you do know you were going twenty-one miles over the speed limit? You should know that's a criminal offense."

Cody winced. "Sorry."

"You're lucky this is a lonely stretch of road and no one else is around." John lowered the clipboard and Cody blew out a breath of relief as his cousin continued, "Watch your speed or next time I'll have to give you a ticket."

"You've got it." Cody gave John an expression of appreciation. "How are Uncle Hal and Aunt Angel?"

"They're both doing well." John seemed to relax as he spoke of his parents. "You missed the reunion on Easter. It was a hell of a good time. You should drop by and see the folks."

"You're right, I should go see them," Cody said. "Really sucked that I got called in on the morning of the reunion—that was one of the days the damned arsonist struck."

"That's right." John gave a nod. "Reese has been keeping me updated on the progress in the case. I heard that one of the victims received a threatening letter, and another one is missing."

"Yeah." Cody frowned. "I don't like this, don't like it at all."

"Same here." John's radio squawked on his shoulder and he responded to it. Cody recognized it was the code for a domestic dispute.

"Watch that speed," John said as he took a step back.

"You bet," Cody said before John turned away.

Cody pulled his truck back onto the road, kept his speed just a couple of miles over the speed limit, and headed the last mile to the turnoff to his home.

The thought of seeing Carilyn again made him smile. He had been looking forward to seeing her again since the day he'd left for his shift. It was the first time he could remember that time had seemed to crawl unbelievably slow.

Carilyn was on the porch swing as he drove up to the house, typing on her laptop as she moved the swing back and forth. She looked up and smiled and gave a little wave to him as he parked.

He smiled and grabbed his duffel as he climbed out. He shut the truck door behind him, and then strode up to the house.

She closed the lid of the laptop and held it in her lap as she waited for him to walk up the porch. Loose tendrils of her red hair had escaped her braid and floated around her face in a soft breeze.

When he reached her, she stood, still holding her laptop as she said, "Good morning."

The thought of having her waiting for him every time he came home from getting off a shift sent warmth through his gut.

He wanted to kiss her, but instead said, "How are you feeling?"

"So much better." She walked in through the doorway as he held the door open for her.

"You wouldn't just be saying that because you want to go to Leigh's?" he said as entered behind her and closed the door behind them.

She shook her head. "Honest."

"You'd better be." His lips quirked as he tossed his duffel on the loveseat. "Or I'll have to turn you over my knee for lying."

She raised her chin in mock indignation. "I am not lying, Mr. McBride." She turned toward the kitchen. "Come on and have some breakfast."

"Smells great," he said as he sniffed the air. It smelled like baked potatoes and cheese. He followed her into the kitchen.

"It's a breakfast casserole." She opened the oven and took out a casserole dish with potholders and set it on the stove. "Hopefully it's not dry. I've been keeping it warm for you. I managed not to burn it."

He grinned. "I bet it's great."

She grabbed a trivet and he carried the casserole to the table. "Only taste will tell," she said.

Over breakfast he described the kids in the second grade class who had come to the fire station. He and the other firefighters had enjoyed the kids' visit and he could tell that Carilyn enjoyed hearing about it. She told him a little about what she'd been doing, but told him overall it was pretty boring compared to having a group of second graders visit.

After breakfast, Cody went outside to take care of chores. He couldn't get Carilyn off his mind. More importantly, he didn't want to get her off his mind.

He was glad to see that she was feeling better. It was clear from the animated way she talked, her smile, and how clear her green eyes were, that she was doing a lot better. The only thing that bothered him was her insistence that she needed to go back to Leigh's. Yes, he was concerned for her safety, but he enjoyed her company and didn't want her to go.

Somehow he had to convince her to stay until they had a better handle on this Firebug thing, or the bastard was caught.

Chapter 14

A sick feeling settled in Carilyn's belly as she walked into Leigh's living room. It looked even worse the second time around. The first time she'd been in shock. Now she was just angry.

"How dare someone do this?" Her voice came out hard.

"I don't like the thought of you staying here." Cody's words were tight. "Like I've said before, the bastard could come back."

She said nothing as she righted a chair and adjusted the couch cushions. Cody helped, too, picking up the pieces of a broken lamp from off the floor.

Carilyn looked at the end table and her skin went cold. The frame that had contained the photo of Leigh, Misha, and herself was empty. The photograph was gone.

"Oh, my God." Carilyn's heart thumped so hard her chest ached. "He was here again."

"What?" Cody was at her side in a couple of strides. "How do you know?"

Carilyn pointed to the frame. "I picked that up off the floor when we were here last. The glass was broken but the photograph was there." She looked at Cody to see anger on his features. "He came back."

"You're not staying here tonight." Cody's eyes were narrowed as he looked at the empty frame. He turned his gaze on Carilyn. "No arguments."

"Believe me, I'm not arguing." She shuddered. "Just knowing he was here again makes me sick inside."

Cody nodded. "I'm calling Reese. Maybe they'll get fingerprints this time."

They didn't touch the frame in case the bastard's fingerprints were on it, and waited for Reese who arrived with a couple of police officers and a forensics specialist.

Once the officers were there, Carilyn went through the house again to see if anything else was disturbed that hadn't been the last time. They didn't know if the emailer, the person who ransacked the house, and the arsonist were related, but Cody searched for any sign that the arsonist could have tampered with the house.

After they were done combing the house, the only thing Carilyn could tell had been touched was the photo. The forensics guy said the frame had been wiped smooth—even Carilyn's fingerprints from when she'd handled it the last time were gone.

When they were finished, the officers left and just Reese remained. "You've received no other contact from Firebug, have you?" he asked Carilyn.

She shook her head. "No."

Reese looked from her to Cody. "No unusual visitors to the ranch?"

"Only Gisele, the mail carrier, and Tom, the ranch hand," Carilyn said. "No one else has come by Cody's ranch since I've been there."

"Have you noticed anything else strange that you can think of?" Reese asked.

"No," Carilyn responded.

"Unknown callers, hang ups?" he asked.

She frowned. The only one to call her had been Sam, and she'd missed his calls. "No one," she said.

Reese looked at Cody who shook his head. Reese finished questioning them and pulled Cody aside. Carilyn wondered what they were talking about, but turned and looked around her at the violation.

Feeling even sicker than before, Carilyn started to clean up the mess again.

Cody rested his hand on her shoulder, startling her. "I don't think we should stay." He met her gaze. "If it's the arsonist, he could target this house."

A helpless feeling weighted down on her as she looked from Cody to Reese. "I don't want Leigh to return home to a mess."

"There's plenty of time," Cody said. "She won't be back for almost a month. By then the police will have caught the bastard."

"I hope you're right." Carilyn blew out her breath. "Let's go."

Reese and Cody made sure all of the doors and windows were locked while she waited for them in the living room. Apparently the back door had been jimmied, so Cody was going to have someone fix it and put on a bolt lock.

She stared at the empty picture frame. Why would the person who ransacked Leigh's home come back for the photo? Cold traveled down her spine again and she shivered.

"Everything's locked up tight." Cody's voice jerked her out of her thoughts and she whirled to face him.

"I wish Leigh had an alarm system," Carilyn said.

"So do I," Cody said grimly.

Reese left with Cody and Carilyn. She gave Reese a little wave as he pulled away in his unmarked vehicle.

They were quiet on the way back to the ranch, Carilyn lost in her thoughts and Cody seemed to be, too.

They were almost to the ranch when he spoke. "Why don't we go out tonight? Jo-Jo's has happy hour 'til seven."

"Okay." Carilyn looked at him. She could use a distraction. "Is Jo-Jo's a bar?"

"Probably the nicest one in Prescott." He smiled. "Although Nectars is classy, too, it's just hard to compare the two."

"I think I saw Nectars when I went to the Hummingbird." She swallowed. "The day my car was burned up."

"Yes, it's right next door." He glanced at her before looking at the road again. "Wasn't planning on taking you there since that's where it happened."

She nodded.

"My cousin, Tate's, wife owns Jo-Jo's," Cody said. "His brother, my cousin Gage's, in-laws own the Hummingbird and Nectars."

Carilyn couldn't help a laugh. "You McBrides do get around."

He grinned and looked at her. "You should see the Johnsons."

* * * * *

Before they left, Carilyn took a long bath to relax and get her mind off of all that had happened. It wasn't easy, but she finally set it aside so that she could enjoy a night out with Cody.

After she had dried off, she dressed in a matching black bra and panty set. She slipped into the sleeveless emerald green dress she had picked out on impulse when she and Leigh had gone shopping. The dress reached a few inches above her knees and she had to admit it looked great on her. She stepped into black strappy heels she'd also picked out that matched a small black purse with a long strap. She brushed out her hair and let it fall around her shoulders. She usually kept it back but today she felt like leaving it down. After she grabbed the purse, she left her room to meet Cody.

"Hello, gorgeous," he said the moment she walked into the living room. Her cheeks heated and she knew she was blushing as he looked at her with appreciation in his gaze. "You always look beautiful."

"Thank you." She smiled at him.

He opened the door for her then touched the small of her back as he escorted her to the truck. Her heels wobbled a little on the uneven ground and he caught her by her upper arm and steadied her. When they reached the truck, he opened the passenger door and helped her up and into the truck, and then closed the door behind her. He went around to the driver's side, climbed in, and started the vehicle.

They chatted on the way to town and Jo-Jo's. Carilyn was looking forward to meeting more of Cody's relatives and friends. From the way Cody talked about his cousins, they seemed like a cohesive family. They had their differences like any family, but they were all fairly close.

She liked when he told stories about his family. It made her feel like she was a part of the town and his life. And as she thought that, she wondered if just maybe she was starting to get too comfortable there and care for Cody too much.

When she grew quiet, Cody said, "Are you all right, Carilyn?"

She nodded and gave him a smile. "Great," she said.

It wasn't too long before they reached town and made it to Jo-Jo's. After parking, they walked into the bar. It was a weeknight, and Cody said it wasn't as crowded as it would be on weekends, but it was still busy.

A tall, leggy, beautiful woman approached them. She had hair that was a darker shade of red than Carilyn's and her figure-hugging sparkling dress was short, showing off her long legs and her gorgeous figure.

"Carilyn, this is Jo Burke McBride," Cody said. "She's married to my cousin, Tate." Cody turned to the woman, "Jo, this is Carilyn Thompson. She's Leigh's friend from Kansas and is staying while Leigh is in Europe."

"Great to meet you." Jo's smile was brilliant. "Welcome to Prescott, and welcome to Jo-Jo's."

Carilyn liked Jo at once. "Your place is great," Carilyn said to Jo. "It looks like you have fun around here."

"That we do." Jo's smile was sensual as she looked at a tall, dark-haired man with green eyes who reached hem. "This is my husband, Tate." In turn she introduced Carilyn to Tate and they shook hands and greeted each other. According to Cody, Jo and Tate were around ten years older than Carilyn and Cody, but they certainly didn't look it to Carilyn.

"Have a seat over here." Jo nodded to a corner. "That's where 'the girls' and I sit whenever we're having a girls' night out."

"That sounds like fun," Carilyn said with a smile.

"The first round of drinks is on the house," Jo said as they reached the table.

When they were seated, a server with a nametag that read "Tanya" arrived and took their drink orders. Dark-haired Tanya had a cute figure and her skirt was almost as short as Jo's dress.

Carilyn decided on a pineapple mojito while Jo ordered a cosmo and the men asked for domestic beers.

They had barely settled in when another cousin and his wife arrived. Garrett and Ricki had just married a few weeks ago.

Carilyn was surprised at how easy it was to not think about Firebug or Leigh's ransacked house or her burned up car…much. A couple of times the thoughts flashed through Carilyn's mind, but she easily slipped back into listening to the cousins and their wives as well as Cody.

After her second mojito, Carilyn excused herself to go to the ladies' room. She headed across the bar and down a hall to the restroom. Five minutes later she opened the restroom door to leave.

As she entered the hallway someone ran into her from behind, almost knocking her off her feet. She braced her hand on a wall to steady herself.

"Are you okay?" A pudgy guy, who looked like a stereotypical geek, moved into her line of vision and peered at her, his hand on her upper arm, a look of concern on his round, bearded features. "Sorry for running into you like that."

With a smile, she said, "No problem. I'm perfectly fine."

"Let me buy you a drink." He looked down at his feet, his longish hair falling into his pale blue eyes. He glanced up again. "It's the least I can do."

"Thanks, but you don't need to do that," she said.

"But I want to." He gave her a pleading look. "Please?"

Feeling uncomfortable with the way he was looking at her, she fixed a smile on her face. "I'm here with someone and he'll miss me if I don't come right back." The man's face fell and Carilyn couldn't help but feel bad. "I appreciate the offer, though."

He nodded. "Yeah, sure." He turned away, headed down the hall and then vanished into the crowd beyond it.

She let out her breath and shook her head. That was weird. She felt bad for some reason, but there was no sense in letting the guy get his hopes up by allowing him to buy a drink for her. It had been clear that he was interested in her beyond trying to make up for running into her.

When she returned to the table, Cody smiled at her. His smile faded a little as she slid into the booth next to him. "What's wrong?"

"Nothing." She gave him a bright smile and pushed thoughts of the geek to the back of her mind. "I'm ready for another mojito."

She had just finished her third mojito when Cody asked her to dance. He took her by the hand and led her to the dance floor. She felt a little tipsy and warm inside but was still steady on her feet.

It was a slow song, and Cody brought her in close to him as she put her hands on his shoulders. A fluttering sensation batted around in her belly and her heart beat a little faster as she felt his body heat even though there was a good inch between them.

His beautiful warm brown eyes studied her. "Enjoying yourself?"

She hoped he couldn't see the sudden nervousness that gripped her. "Yes. I like your cousins and their wives."

The corner of his mouth tipped up. "There's plenty more where they came from."

She smiled in return and he brought her in closer so that their bodies were touching and she caught her breath. She linked her hands around his neck as he moved his own hands to her hips.

Heat rose inside her and her throat grew dry as their gazes held. He looked at her lips as if he wanted to kiss her. She wanted him to more than she'd ever wanted a kiss before. Her tongue darted out to touch her lips and he brought her body flush with his.

The hard ridge of his erection pressed against her belly. An ache grew between her thighs and her nipples grew taut. She had the sudden desire to take him by the hand, lead him out of the club, and tell him to drive home as fast as possible.

She wanted him. And she wanted him now.

Someone ran into her from behind and she fell forward against Cody. She looked over her shoulder but the couples around them seemed to be paying attention only to their partners. It was the second time that night that someone had run into her, but this time there wasn't a guy trying to apologize to her.

"Don't get me wrong," Cody said as she looked back at him. He was grinning as he held her tight. "But you don't have to throw yourself at me."

Heat warmed her cheeks. "Someone bumped into me."

He just smiled, a slow sensual smile that curled her toes.

The slow song was winding down and she didn't want it to stop. Without realizing that she was doing it, she moved up onto her tiptoes and he lowered his head.

When his lips met hers, it was like fireworks went off in her belly and in her mind. Vaguely she was aware that a faster tune had started playing, but still Cody kissed her. It was a long, slow kiss that sent thrills from where their lips met straight to her toes.

She was breathing hard when they parted and she looked into his eyes that glittered in the low lighting.

His throat worked as he held her gaze. "Ready to go home?" His voice was husky.

She only hesitated a moment before she gave a single nod. He put his palm on her lower back and guided her through the crowd of dancers and back to where the others were sitting and laughing about something.

Cody paid the tab with Tanya, and then he and Carilyn walked to Jo's table as he held Carilyn's hand. His touch was warm and electric and she loved the feel of her smaller hand in his larger one.

"We're taking off, Jo," Cody said as she stood.

Jo hugged him then Carilyn. "It was great to meet you," Jo said as she drew away from Carilyn.

"Thank you for the hospitality." Carilyn smiled.

Tate, Garrett, and Ricki also stood and hugged Carilyn as if she was a part of the family.

When they turned to leave, Cody took her hand again and squeezed it. She looked up at him and smiled as they headed through the front entrance.

Chapter 15

Cody held Carilyn's hand on the console as he drove back to the ranch. His hand was warm over hers and she turned her palm up and linked her fingers with his.

"How are you doing?" His tone was low and rough as he spoke.

"Good." Her own voice was husky with desire.

Maybe she'd had too much to drink…those three mojitos had been strong. But she knew that wasn't the reason why she wanted Cody so much. She'd wanted him from the first moment she saw him at the Hummingbird.

The sexual tension between them was electric. She could feel it arcing through their hands and traveling through her body like fire.

When they reached the ranch, Cody parked then jumped out and hurried around the truck to help her down. Her dress crept up her thighs as she got out and he looked at her bared thighs and he gripped her tighter. Her dress slid back down when her feet met the ground and his gaze met hers again.

"Come on, honey." He clasped her hand in his as he shut the truck door.

She gripped her purse in one hand and his hand in the other. The sexual tension increased as they went through the front door and he shut the door hard behind them.

The next thing she knew, her back was against the door, his body pressing hard, and his mouth taking hers. She moaned and kissed him back, wrapping her arms around his neck. Her mind whirled and she felt almost dizzy from the intensity of the kiss.

He groaned as he grabbed her ass and brought her even tighter to him. Her dress slid up to her waist, exposing her black panties, as she hooked her thighs around his hips. Her breathing came fast and hard as she kissed him with everything she had.

When he drew away, his chest rose and fell as he held her tight to him. "Tell me to stop," he said as he looked down at her. "Last chance."

"No," she said. "I don't want you to stop."

A low growl rose up in his throat and he started to carry her down the hall toward the master bedroom. She buried her face against his neck and kissed it, tasting his saltiness while drawing in his scent. He smelled so good and his arms were so big and strong as they held her.

He carried her into the room and set her on her feet on the rug beside the bed. "I could just eat you up, sweetheart. All of you."

"Do it." She kicked off her shoes as he toed off his boots and shoved them aside. He reached for the zipper on her dress. "Take all of me."

He growled again as he pulled down the zipper, she grabbed the collar of his western shirt and pulled the pearl snaps apart so that the shirt opened all the way down to his waist. She shoved his shirt over his shoulders and he shrugged it off in a fast movement before flinging his shirt aside.

Their movements were almost frantic as they undressed each other. It was as if all the moments they'd been together, never touching but wanting, had combined into a need so great that they couldn't control themselves.

Her dress slid over her skin, landing around her feet and she stepped out of it. He reached behind her and unhooked her bra before sliding the straps down her arms and tossing it aside. He pushed her panties down, leaving her naked.

"Damn but your skin is soft." He ran his callused palms over her bared skin. "I want to touch every bit of you. I want to taste every inch."

She swallowed. "I want it all."

Sensual promise was in his eyes. "I'm going to give you everything." Then he lowered his head and sucked her nipples. She gasped and dug her fingers into his shoulders as he nipped at and licked her sensitive nipples until he was about to drive her out of her mind.

Their mouths met in a clash as she fumbled for the button on his Wrangler jeans then unzipped them. She shoved his jeans down his hips, followed by his boxer briefs. His cock was warm and hard in her palm as she grasped it. He groaned as she rubbed her thumb over the head and spread the drop of semen.

He shoved his jeans the rest of the way down along with the boxer briefs and she had to release him when he stripped off his socks, too. As soon as he was fully naked, she grasped his cock again. He reached for her but she dropped to her knees in front of him.

"Carilyn." Cody uttered her name in a hoarse whisper as he buried his fingers in her hair. "Let me take care of you," he said, but she seemed entirely focused on him and didn't listen.

He felt helpless to do anything but let her take control. His entire body was strung tight as she lowered her head and slipped his cock into her mouth. He groaned as he felt her hot mouth sliding over his erection.

She kept taking him, deeper and deeper until he was all the way to the back of her throat. He'd never felt anything like her mouth on him, the way she took him deep, the way she sucked on him at the same time.

"Damn, sweetheart." He groaned then cupped the back of her head and pushed down. She looked up at him as she took him deep before pulling back and then going down on him again. Her eyes were heavy-lidded, her look so sensual that he wondered if he'd come from just looking into her eyes and at her naked body as she knelt in front of him. Her breasts were perfect, her nipples hard.

A climax spiraled closer and closer as she moved her mouth up and down on him and he gritted his teeth. He came close to coming and gripped her hair, keeping her still for a moment.

"Hold on," he said through gritted teeth. "I'm close to coming." She waited until he let his breath out and he pushed her down.

When she started again, she held his cock in one hand and moved it up and down in time with her mouth. With her other hand she grasped his balls and gripped them tight as if tethering him to her.

He felt the climax coming on again and this time he didn't think he was going to be able to hold himself back. He clenched his fist in her hair again, holding her still as he pulled his cock out of her mouth.

She looked up at him and licked her lips and he groaned again. He bent and grasped her by her upper arms and brought her to her feet. He kissed her hard, loving the way she kissed him in return with a kind of passion he'd never experienced before. He wanted her in so many ways, ways that he'd never imagined wanting anyone, ever.

Her body felt warm against his as he held her tightly to him. He gripped her ass in his hands, her flesh so soft to his touch. He caught her up in his arms, picked her up, and laid her on the bed quilt. He watched her as he moved onto the bed and pushed her thighs apart with his hands.

Carilyn looked down at Cody between her thighs, her heart beating fast as their eyes met. He kissed the insides of her thighs, his lips warm and feathery against her soft flesh.

Her heart pounded faster as she watched him lower his head, his mouth hovering over her sex. He blew on her clit, causing her to gasp and her eyes to widen. The sensation heightened her anticipation, her throat dry as she waited for him to go down on her. He seemed to know that he was causing her body to be strung as tight as a bow and he was doing everything he could to string her even tighter.

The moment she felt his mouth on her, she arched, throwing her head back and she nearly came up off the bed. He ran his tongue along her folds and then flicked it over her clit. She moaned as she looked down again to see his dark head between her thighs. The sight of him there, his big shoulders pressing her thighs farther apart, made the sensations all the more intense.

His eyes met hers as he raised his head. "You taste so good," he said in a low rumble, his words sending thrill after thrill throughout her. "I can't wait to eat you all up."

She cried out as he slid two fingers inside her. He moved them in and out in slow motion as he lowered his head and licked her again. She moaned as she gripped the quilt in her fists, her knuckles aching from grasping it so tightly.

He thrust his fingers in and out as he licked and sucked her. Every breath she took came faster and harder as she felt an orgasm approaching fast.

"Stop—stop. I'm going to come." She squirmed but he gripped her hips in his big hands and wouldn't let her move away from him.

She tried to hold back but she couldn't stop the climax rushing toward her. Faster and faster it thundered through her. His tongue was magic and seeing him watching her while he licked and sucked her made her orgasm come closer even faster.

A cry escaped her that she couldn't hold back as she came off of the bed, coming hard. She felt her mind spinning and spinning as he continued to lick and suck her and her body bucked again from the aftershocks. Blood roared in her ears and she shivered from the impact of her orgasm.

And then he was moving up on the bed as she tried to pull her thoughts back together. They seemed scattered, as if she'd never gather them back again.

She watched as he rolled a condom down his cock and she felt a thrill low in her belly, knowing that he was going to be inside her in moments. She wanted that more than anything.

He placed the head of his cock against her center and she found herself holding her breath. He put his hands on hers to either side of her head, and linked their fingers together, gripping her tightly.

From what she saw in his expression, he seemed to be losing his control too, unable to hold himself back. He thrust hard, driving into her, burying himself deep inside. She cried out in surprise at the sudden entry and at the feel of him stretching her.

He began moving in and out of her, pulling out almost all of the way and then plunging in hard again. She arched her hips up to meet this every thrust as he drove in and out, fucking her out of her mind.

Sweat beaded on his forehead and she felt perspiration on her own body as they moved together as one. The intensity was so great that her mind was whirling, her thoughts flying. Her body was rushing toward another orgasm, even faster than before.

A cry ripped from her throat as she climaxed again. Hot tears rolled down the sides of her face as her body shook and trembled.

It was all too intense, too much, and she could barely hold onto reality. Her body vibrated as he continued to take her, her core spasming around his cock. Every movement he made was almost too much for her to bear.

She felt like her mind was floating away from her body, everything was so incredible, so unbelievably powerful. Spots flickered in front of her eyes and she wondered for a moment if she was going to lose consciousness.

As she looked into his eyes, she worked to reel her thoughts back in. His expression was fierce, like some proud warrior. She would have thought he was angry if she didn't know better. It was like he was as on fire as she was, burning even hotter and brighter.

He shouted her name as he moved in and out of her several more times. She felt his cock throbbing inside her as his climax took him to even greater heights. She could see unmistakable pleasure in his eyes, pleasure that bordered on the verge of pain. She knew how he felt because it had been the same for her.

His body shuddered and then he collapsed against her. He barely held all of his weight off of her. His thick, muscular body was hot and slick against hers. She wriggled beneath him, loving the feel of his cock still inside her and the heat of his body.

He brought his mouth to hers and kissed her hard before moving off of her. He brought her into his arms, holding her close. "I'm never letting you go," he murmured.

Despite the promise in his words and her own misgivings, she snuggled against him, feeling as if in that moment they had become one. He stroked her hair away from her face and rested his chin on top of her head. She gave a happy little sigh and drifted off to sleep in his arms.

CHAPTER 16

Nathan scowled as he stared at his computer, not really seeing the screen as his thoughts raced. At the bar Carilyn Thompson had rejected him, just like every one of the other three women. Who did Carilyn think she was, anyway? God's gift to men?

That Cody McBride was a real problem. Not only was he in the way with Carilyn, but he was working to catch the arsonist… and what if he was close?

Nathan needed to take care of McBride before he got too close. Nathan had made sure the first arson investigator had been injured severely enough that he'd been forced off the job. Nathan would have to more than hurt McBride to get him out of the way.

He could arrange for McBride to die. That would fix everything.

Nathan's stomach felt queasy as he thought about Janice's body. His first kill.

Killing Janice had been easier than he'd thought. Would McBride be just as easy? All Nathan had to do was make sure

McBride was in the right place at the right time—meaning right for Nathan, wrong for McBride.

He thought about sending another email to Carilyn. He could send something that would really unnerve her. But should he hold back, lulling her into a false sense of security? As much as he wanted to torch them all, biding his time might be the best thing he could do for now.

With an angry brush of his hand, he pushed his hair out of his eyes and stood so fast that he knocked his chair over. It hit the floor with a hard thump. He held still for a moment, hoping that old hag, Mrs. Richter, hadn't heard. He couldn't afford drawing attention to himself and she took every opportunity to stick her long nose into his business.

Maybe he should kill the witch. He gave a smirk at the thought of lighting that bag of bones on fire. If it weren't for the fact that it would mean losing his own home, he'd burn up her place too. Of course he also couldn't afford to kill her because the police would likely be banging on his door while searching for the hag if she turned up missing.

It surprised him how easily he was thinking about killing now. It was a line he hadn't known he could ever cross… But now that he had, it would be easier to do it again.

Nathan's cell phone rang, jolting him out of his thoughts. He pulled it out of his pocket and looked at the screen. Of course it was his mother. No one else called him.

"Hi, Ma." He tried to inject a little enthusiasm in his voice, but it wasn't easy. With her health failing, it tore at him every time he talked with her. Even after all she'd done, he still loved her. "How are you doing?"

"Not so good." Aggie sounded sour. "Why haven't you come to see me?"

"I will, Ma," he said. "Soon, I promise."

Her tone was sharp. "You haven't bothered to come here for a while. You don't give a damn about me."

"I love you, Ma," he hurried to say. "It's only been two weeks."

"Only two weeks?" The shrillness of her response made him wince.

"I'm sorry." He knew better than to make excuses and he knew better than to stay away so long. He just hated to see her looking so sickly and he hated visiting the rest home with all the sick old people in it. "I'll be there this weekend. I promise."

"What did I do to deserve a boy who doesn't care about his own mother?" She grew even shriller.

A sick feeling settled in his belly. "I love you, Ma," he said again. "I'll see you Saturday."

"I don't feel so well." Now she sounded pathetic, as if the energy she'd expended yelling at him had weakened her. "I need to lie down."

"I'll see you in a few days," he said before she hung up.

Heart heavy, Nathan headed to the table where his scrapbook was open with his latest find front and center, and he pushed away thoughts of his mother.

It had been a risk, but he'd gone back to Leigh's house to get the picture of Carilyn with Leigh and some other slut. He'd grabbed it on his first trip there but had set it down and forgot to take it with him until he was already home, but he hadn't dared to go back right away. He ran his finger along the edge of the picture as he wondered if Carilyn had noticed the photo was missing when she went back.

He glanced at a TV monitor next to his computer. He had mounted a camera across the street from Leigh's house, on a neighbor's home, aimed at Leigh's front door. Carilyn had finally shown up again today…unfortunately it had been with McBride.

He'd thought of booby-trapping the house to go up in flames if anyone came back, but that wasn't personal enough. No, he planned on having some one-on-one time with Carilyn.

Perverse pleasure had him flipping through the pages of his scrapbook again. He found the page with the picture of Janice just moments before he had fried her. He liked seeing her tied up, fear in her eyes while he set the Barbie beside her. At that moment he hadn't intended on killing her, but it had happened and he couldn't say he was sorry.

It was almost a shame no one would ever see the scrapbook. It was filled with so much detail that he felt a lump of pride in his throat every time he looked at it. Each step he'd taken was well-documented. He loved looking over the details of his triumphs and reliving every precious moment.

With each page he flipped through, his smile broadened. The beauty of the fires he had set was enough to bring tears to his eyes. In each photo, he could almost see the lovely orange and blue flames dancing, hear the crackle and hiss as the fire burned, feel the caressing heat, and smell the acrid odor of the smoke. Beautiful.

He reached Carilyn's section. In the photos, her hair looked like flame against her pale skin. In one image she was watching her car as it burned. The look of shock on her face made her somehow even more beautiful to him.

In contrast, the photo with her, Leigh, and the other woman showed a happy Carilyn with laughter in her eyes. What had she been thinking when that picture had been taken? About some dick boyfriend?

He scowled. He couldn't wait to teach her a lesson when he had her all to himself.

When he got to watch her burn.

CHAPTER 17

"I had no idea that Arizona has a wine country," Carilyn said to Cody as he helped her into the wine tour company's black Excursion SUV limousine in front of the Hummingbird. She had never been in an SUV limo before, and she was amazed at how large an interior it had and how luxurious the butter-soft leather seating was.

"There are vineyards and wineries across the state." Cody settled into the seat next to her as the limo driver closed the door behind him. "I thought you might enjoy a tour of our wine country."

"I'm sure I will." She smiled as she opened the brochure the driver had given her. "This says, 'according to the *Wall Street Journal*, the Verde Valley is an emerging hotspot vying for Napa-like status.'"

"It's been some time since I've been on one of these tours." Cody glanced out of the window as the limo started to move. "The last time I went was a few years ago with a good-sized group."

"This is my first time on any wine tour," Carilyn said. "Do we have this huge limo all to ourselves?"

"I know the owner." He shifted in his seat and grinned. "Let's just say she gave me a great deal."

It was the day after Cody had worked another forty-eight hour shift. They had just eaten an early brunch at the Hummingbird in anticipation of a day touring the wine country.

Cody put his arm around her shoulders and she snuggled next to him before tipping her face up to look at him. He kissed her, soft and sweet and when he drew back he smiled.

Ever since the night they'd spent together in each other's arms, their relationship had changed. At first Carilyn had been concerned about starting a relationship with Cody, after all, she lived so far away. Now, she still was concerned, but she'd decided to enjoy their time together and not worry about a little something like distance.

A part of her felt that wasn't fair to either one of them, but she couldn't get herself to put a halt to it. She was attracted to him far too much.

While she relaxed against Cody, she watched as the scenery sped by. It wasn't long before they reached Old Town Cottonwood and the first winery. It was a quaint town and the winery was exclusive with a tasting room that was furnished in rich woods and soft leather.

Carilyn was glad she'd worn something tasteful yet casual, and she felt comfortable around other guests at the winery. As much as she'd traveled, she'd never become a fine wine connoisseur.

Cody taught her to swirl her wine in the glass to aerate the wine's myriad aromas and to inhale deeply before taking a sip. She then swirled the wine in her mouth to pick up different flavor and texture combinations.

She learned to select the lighter wines first, before heavier and bolder wines, saving sweet wines for last. She admitted to Cody that her favorite wines were the sweeter ones. Wine tasting etiquette allowed for either swallowing the wine after tasting or spitting it into a spittoon. If she drank too much while tasting the wines, she would end up without a clear head, so she tended to swallow only her favorites of those she tasted.

In between each wine she sampled different kinds of cheeses and crackers, two of her favorite kinds of food.

After visiting the first two wineries, it was time for lunch. They were provided a picnic lunch to enjoy on a deck overlooking Oak Creek. The artisan sandwiches were delicious and she enjoyed the cool air and the smell of the trees, along with Cody's great company.

When they were finished with lunch, the limo driver took them to Page Springs where they stopped at two more wineries. While they traveled between wineries, they talked about their day-to-day lives before they had met. Because she worked out of her home, her days could be lonely, so she did what she could to get out of the house. Still, she didn't really get out enough. Cody's quiet time tended to be when he was on the ranch, away from town and the fire department.

That evening, the limo rolled into Prescott, taking them back to the Hummingbird. It had been an amazing day and Carilyn hadn't felt that happy in a long time. She'd enjoyed every moment she'd spent with Cody during the day, and looked forward to being with him alone at his home when they returned.

After they stepped out of the limo, Cody turned to tip the driver. Carilyn stood on the sidewalk, a breeze stirring the loose tendrils of her hair around her face. She absently brushed strands out of her eyes but went still when a prickle traveled down her spine.

Someone was watching her.

She whirled and looked behind her. No one anywhere in sight. Feeling unnerved, she searched her surroundings with her gaze but saw nothing out of the ordinary. Two women walked out of an antique shop, chatting animatedly while someone turned the "Open" sign to "Closed" behind them.

In the distance she noticed a man striding down the street, his back to her. She hadn't seen him until this moment, but something about him seemed familiar, like she'd seen him someplace before. She knew very few people in Prescott, including some of Cody's relatives and the firefighters she'd met when her car burned up and at the fire station.

Even though she was seeing the man from his backside, this guy seemed to have a different bearing, a different walk, than anyone she'd met—that she could remember. He was hunched over, his hands shoved into his pockets.

She moved her gaze away from the retreating man and searched the street for a sign of anyone else. No one.

A hand gripped her upper arm and she startled. She looked to see Cody as he smiled and slid his arm around her shoulders. "Ready to go back to the ranch, sunshine?"

The limo was pulling away from the curb as she let out her breath and nodded. "You didn't swallow much, so you're all right to drive?"

He gently tugged on a strand of her hair and gave her a smile. "Exactly. The last bit I had was a couple of hours ago."

She rested her head against him as they walked to where he'd parked his truck. "I think I had enough for both of us today," she said. "You could say that I'm feeling very relaxed right now."

Even as they walked off together, she still felt unnerved despite being relaxed. She had no reason to feel that way, but she did.

Yet, then again, her car had been torched, she had received a threatening email, and Leigh's house had been tossed. So yeah, she did have a reason to feel that way. With their day in the wine country, she'd let all that worry slide away and she had just enjoyed herself. Now it was back to reality.

She frowned to herself as she thought about the fact that she hadn't tracked down the guy who'd threatened her via email. He'd covered his tracks very well. She was going to have to call in favors if she didn't find him soon.

"What's wrong?" Cody's concerned voice jerked her out of her thoughts. "You look like something's bothering you."

She gave him a bright smile. "Like I said, I'm relaxed from all of that wine."

There was no need to bring up the arsonist and whoever was threatening her and the person or persons who had ransacked Leigh's home. She wondered if they could all be the same person. It would make sense if it were.

Cody helped her into the passenger side before closing the door and going to the driver's side and climbing in. The drive to his home didn't seem to take too long. For most of the drive she was lost in her own thoughts and was glad that he didn't press her to talk.

It was early evening when they arrived at the ranch. Cody left to take care of the chores while Carilyn headed into the house.

The moment she stepped into Cody's darkened home and closed the front door behind her, her skin crawled. Something wasn't right.

She froze, her breath catching in her throat. She backed up against the door and fumbled for the door handle behind her.

No one was here—she was being stupid. She thought of turning on the lights and checking the house, but remained right where she was. If someone was in the house, she could be walking right into a trap.

Jeez, she was being so dramatic. She'd seen way too much TV, that's for sure. There wasn't an ax murderer waiting in the cellar.

But there might just be an arsonist hiding in the house.

Something creaked. She had to get out of there. She gripped the door handle behind her and it clicked as she opened it. Her heart pounded as she tried to pull the door open without putting her back to the room. As soon as she had the door wide enough, she turned and ran out of the house, into the growing darkness.

It felt as if someone was chasing her, but when she looked over the shoulder no one was there.

She looked forward just in time to smack into something solid. She nearly screamed as hands grabbed her by her upper arms.

"Carilyn." It was Cody who had a grip on her. "What's wrong?"

Her whole body felt weak, as if only his hold kept her knees from going out. "I—" She took a deep breath. "It's nothing. I just got spooked is all."

He frowned. "What spooked you?"

She looked over her shoulder at the house again before meeting his gaze again. "I had the feeling that someone's in the house. Or at least someone was."

Cody's features hardened. "Are you certain?"

She shook her head. "I had just set foot in the house before I turned and ran. I thought I heard a noise but it could just have been the wind or something."

"The wind isn't blowing, it's only a breeze." Cody looked grim. "I'm going to check it out."

"What if someone *is* in there?" Carilyn felt panic crawling up her throat. It was irrational, but she couldn't shake the feeling something was wrong. "Don't go."

"I'll be fine, sweetheart." He squeezed her shoulders before taking her by one arm and steering her toward the passenger door of his vehicle. "Get in the truck, lock the doors, and wait for me."

He opened the door and helped her inside. When she was seated, he reached into the glove compartment and she caught her breath as he pulled out a handgun. He gave her a quick look before shutting the door and using the remote in his pocket to lock her in the truck.

She gripped her hands into fists and watched him walk toward the house.

Satisfied that Carilyn was safe for now, Cody gripped his pistol in both hands like his cousin Reese had showed him years ago when Cody had been twelve and Reese had taught Cody how to shoot. He walked up to the front door and opened it, letting the door swing open and stepping to the side. He reached in, flipped on the lights, and waited a moment before clearing the room.

He systematically searched each room in the house but found nothing until he reached the master bedroom.

On the bed was a glass wool tube like the ones they'd found at the first three fires—the tubes that contained Barbies.

"Shit." Cody's heart slammed in his chest as he saw the black box with wires next to the tube.

Adrenaline pumped through his body as he turned and bolted out of the bedroom. He yanked the front door wide, tore through the opening, and ran.

He had almost reached the truck when the world exploded.

Heat rushed toward him. Debris pelted his body.

Something slammed against his head and he dropped. The brilliant orange sky faded and went dark.

CHAPTER 18

Carilyn screamed as the house exploded.

She watched in horror as Cody dropped to the ground.

An object slammed into the truck's windshield, smashing it on the driver's side and she screamed again.

Debris rained from the sky as the house was consumed by fire. She paused a moment as she waited for the worst of it to fall. She opened the vehicle's passenger door, climbed out, and ran toward Cody who was sprawled face down on the ground just feet from the truck.

"Cody!" Blood pounded in her ears as she dropped beside him and shook his shoulder. "Are you all right? Cody, please."

The fire lit up the night and she could see that his hair looked wet behind his head. With a trembling hand, she reached out and touched the wet spot. Her fingers came back coated in blood and she barely kept from screaming again. Forcing herself to breathe, she checked his throat for a pulse and found one. She didn't have any medical training, but it seemed like a solid pulse and it had been easy to find.

Struggling to keep panic at bay, she looked at the fire eating up the night, felt the heat, and tried not to breathe in the acrid smoke. What had happened?

The answer came to her despite the fear clouding her mind. The arsonist had blown up Cody's house. How could it be anything else?

Her skin went cold despite the heat of the fire. What if the arsonist was still here? She felt like she was going to hyperventilate and she forced herself to calm down. She had to think of Cody and not worry about shadows and what ifs.

She looked back at Cody and then at the truck. With no one there, she needed to take him to the hospital but the driver's side of the windshield was smashed in. Leigh's car was next to Cody's truck. Somehow she was going to have to drag his body to the car and get him into it.

How was she going to do that? He was over six feet and around two hundred pounds of dead weight.

She clenched her jaw. She was just going to have to do it.

The fire roared like a beast as she grabbed Cody beneath his arms and tried to drag him. He was too heavy. Clenching her teeth she tried again, and managed to move him a few feet. Her back strained, her arms ached. She grunted and dragged him closer to the car.

She lowered him as it occurred to her that she needed to dial 9-1-1. She'd been so freaked out, so intent on getting him away from there that she hadn't been thinking straight.

Just as she reached for her phone, lights blinded her.

For a moment she was frozen in place, like a deer caught in headlights. What if it was the arsonist? She dodged beside the car so that it was between her and the bright lights.

Spots danced in front of her eyes as she regained her sight. What was happening?

Voices came from the other side of the car and she jerked her attention toward the sound.

"Do you think Cody's in there, Clint?" a woman called out in a frantic voice.

"I saw someone over by the car, Ella," the man named Clint shouted. "Let me have a look while you call 9-1-1."

"All right," Ella said. "Be careful."

Clint—that was Cody's brother's name, and Ella was his fiancée. Her mind spun. Carilyn shook off the dazed feeling and scrambled to her feet. "Over here," she called out. "Cody's over here."

A big form came toward her and then a man was kneeling beside Cody who was still facedown on the ground.

"Cody." The man rested his hand on Cody's neck as he looked up at Carilyn. "I'm Clint, Cody's brother. What happened?"

"The house exploded and something hit him in the head." Tears started flowing down her cheeks. "Is he going to be okay?"

"His pulse is strong." Clint reaffirmed her conclusion. "But any damage beyond his head wound, I couldn't tell you."

She nodded, more tears flowing down her face. "I tried to get him to the car, but he's too big."

"Ella is calling emergency." Clint looked grim. "We're a good distance out of town so it'll take a little longer for the paramedics to get here."

"What if that's too late?" Carilyn's voice quivered.

Clint reached out and rested his hand on Carilyn's shoulder. "He's going to be all right. My little brother is one tough hombre." He squeezed her shoulder. "What's your name?"

She swallowed. "Carilyn. I'm—I'm staying with Cody."

"We saw the explosion from the road when we were near." Clint glanced at the fire. "Do you know what happened?"

She started to shake her head then paused. "It might have been an arsonist who's been setting fires around town."

Clint frowned. "Why do you think that?"

She pushed strands of hair from her eyes. "We think he's after me." She glanced toward the fire. "When I went into the house, I thought someone might be there. Cody had me wait in the truck while he went in to check it out." More tears flooded her cheeks and she hiccupped a sob. "A few minutes later he came tearing out of the house right before it exploded."

Clint looked grim then glanced down at Cody who was stirring. Clint tore off his western shirt, rolled it up, and laid it on the ground. "Let's get him turned over."

She swiped at her tears with the back of her hand then arranged the shirt behind Cody's head like a pillow as they turned him onto his back.

Clint looked over his shoulder as a petite blonde in western jeans and a light blue blouse came toward them. "ETA, Ella?" he asked.

Ella knelt beside Cody. "Fifteen minutes."

"Carilyn, this is Ella, my fiancée." He nodded toward Carilyn. "This is Carilyn. She's staying with Cody."

Ella nodded. "Not exactly the best circumstances to meet."

"No, definitely not," Carilyn said.

Cody groaned and his eyes fluttered open. Nerves tickled Carilyn's belly.

"What the hell?" Cody's gaze met Carilyn's and he frowned and tried to get up. "Are you okay?"

"Don't move." She sniffled. "You're the one who's hurt."

Clint rested his hand on Cody's shoulder, keeping him from getting up and drawing his attention. "Settle on down, little brother."

"Clint?" Cody's expression changed to one of anger as he shoved off his brother's hand. "That bastard. He could still be here."

"So it was the arsonist?" Carilyn asked as Cody sat up. "You're sure?"

He looked a little unsteady but nodded. "Positive." Both Cody and Clint looked at the burning house. "There goes everything we had left from Mom and Dad," Cody said.

"You've still got the rest of the ranch," Ella said.

Clint squeezed Cody's shoulder. "Material possessions are all that were lost. What's important is that you and Carilyn are alive."

Cody looked at Carilyn. "If something had happened to you—" His words cut off, his voice sounding broken.

"Nothing did." She put her hand over his. "We're both okay."

He narrowed his gaze at the fire. "That was laptop number three."

"I don't care about that." She shook her head. "I'm just grateful you're alive."

He turned his hand up and linked his fingers with hers. "I'm going to get him, Carilyn. He's not going to get away with this."

"Shhh." She pushed hair from Cody's brow. "Don't worry about that for now."

Sirens cut the air in the distance. "Calvary is almost here," Clint said as he looked in the direction of the road.

It didn't take long before two fire trucks, three sheriff's department vehicles, and an ambulance arrived at the house. Carilyn couldn't tell if she'd met any of the firefighters before, with it being dark and with their fire gear on.

Soon the scene was well-organized chaos.

Ella directed the paramedics to Cody as the firefighters started battling the blaze.

"I'm okay." At first Cody tried to brush off the paramedics' attention but Carilyn and Clint managed to get Cody to sit still for them.

"They're just doing their job," Clint said. "You remember how that goes?"

"It's true that doctors make the worst patients," Ella said. "I think that goes for firefighters and paramedics, too."

Cody scowled. "We don't have time for this. That bastard is out there."

Carilyn reached out and touched his hand. "We'll find him." She gave him a determined look. "I'll track him down once I get another laptop."

"Bastard," Cody muttered again as the paramedics helped him to the ambulance where he sat and let them attend to his injuries. In the darkness, Carilyn hadn't noticed all of the cuts and splinters in his skin from the explosion.

Like Carilyn had, Cody refused to go to the hospital, insisting it was just a mild concussion and a bump on the head.

"You were out for a while," Clint said.

"A good ten minutes." Carilyn wiped a smudge of dirt from his cheek. "Now we have matching concussions and head wounds."

Cody put his palm on her back and gently rubbed it as he looked into her eyes. "Thank God the explosives didn't go off when you were in the house. I don't know what I'd do if something happened to you."

"I feel that way about you, too." She swallowed. "We were both fortunate."

He leaned forward and kissed her, a gentle kiss, before he drew away again. For a long moment they looked into each other's eyes, neither of them saying a word.

Ella drew their attention. "You can both stay with Clint and me."

Cody shook his head. "I'm not going to put you into danger like that. As long as that arsonist is out there, he could come after us again."

Ella frowned as Clint came up to her side. "What will you do?"

"We'll check into a hotel." Cody dragged his hand down his face.

"That would cost a fortune over the long term," Ella said.

"Not if we find him soon." He had a determined expression. "And we will find him."

Reese joined the group gathered around Cody. Reese looked angry. "How are you doing?" He cut his gaze from Cody to Carilyn.

"Fine." Cody got up from his seat and swayed.

Clint pushed Cody back down. "Isn't this the sheriff department's jurisdiction, not Prescott PD's, cousin?" Clint asked Reese.

"We'll be working together on this one," Reese said. "I'm going to put this bastard behind bars."

Carilyn looked around them. The ground was muddy—the firefighters had apparently used hoses from the stock tanks and they'd managed to keep the fire from spreading to the one nearby structure, a storage shed. The other structures, including the barn and corrals, were a good distance away.

Her throat worked and she swallowed down a lump as she stared at the fire that was still raging. It looked eerie in the night, like some great, fiery beast.

She and Cody could have been in there. The thought that they could have died kept whirling through her mind.

Her knees wobbled and the next thing she knew Cody was drawing her onto his lap. She wrapped her arms around his neck and rested her head against his chest. He held her close and all she knew was that she never wanted to let go.

CHAPTER 19

By the time Cody and Carilyn had checked into a hotel, it was early morning and they hadn't had any sleep. They collapsed on the bed after undressing and taking showers.

Carilyn passed out from exhaustion. She hadn't planned to sleep because someone needed to check on Cody every hour and she was that person.

When she woke, she blinked and stared around the darkened room in confusion. Where she was gradually eased into her consciousness as she noticed a sliver of light peeking through a gap in the hotel room's blackout shades.

Horror drained the blood from her body as the memory of last night slammed into her. The explosion, fire, *Cody*.

She bolted upright on the bed. The sheet fell to her waist. All she wore were black panties and a black bra.

Cody was lying on his side, facing her. The bed sheet draped his hips, his chest bare. Her back had been to him as she slept.

Scratched and bruised, he looked slightly pale, his eyes closed, and her heart squeezed. She reached out and touched his face, her hand shaking. Was he all right?

His flesh was warm beneath her touch. "Wake up, Cody." Her words came out in a hoarse whisper. She cleared her throat and raised her voice as she shook his shoulder. "Cody. Come on. Wake up."

Relief flooded her when his eyelids raised and he met her gaze. "Hey, sunshine," he said in a groggy voice with a faint smile.

She managed a smile, too. "How are you?"

"I've been better." He put his hand over hers where it rested on his cheek. "What about you?"

"Good." She frowned. "I should have stayed awake and watched out for you."

"I'm fine." He squeezed her hand as he scooted up in bed beside her. "I don't think my concussion is as bad as yours was."

She tilted her head to the side. "Now how would you know that?"

"I've had a couple of concussions before and this one doesn't seem nearly as bad," he said.

She relaxed. "I'm so glad."

He reached up and stroked the side of her face as he looked at her intently. "I don't know what I would have done if anything had happened to you. I'm in love with you, Carilyn. You're a part of me now."

She stared at him as his words sank in. "You love me?"

"More than you can imagine." He nodded. "I've never felt this way about anyone before."

Her mind whirled. She couldn't believe what he'd just told her. But she was leaving…

His smile was almost a little sad as he took her face in his palms and leaned close to kiss her. When their lips met it was the sweetest kiss she could ever have imagined.

As he drew away, he looked at her with such love in his eyes that it melted her heart and soul. "Let me show you." He reached behind her and unfastened her bra and she let him slide the straps down her arms.

She shivered beneath his gaze as he cupped her breasts in his palms. He lightly flicked her nipples with his thumbs and she bit her lower lip. He leaned toward her and kissed her again before taking her into his arms.

"You are so beautiful in so many ways," he said as he shifted her and laid her on her back, her head resting on his pillow.

She looked up at him, her heart pounding harder. He hooked his fingers in the waistband of her panties and tugged them down, leaving her bared to his gaze.

He shed his boxers and she watched the play of his muscles as he moved. His naked body was so powerful and he had a day's growth of stubble on his jaws.

One thought dominated her mind. Cody was hers. *Hers.*

And she belonged to him.

All other thought fled her mind. What mattered was that they were together and they were alive. They both could have died tonight.

"I don't want to ever be without you." His words echoed her thoughts.

"I'm here, Cody." She reached out to him and he took her into his arms.

His big body was so warm and hard against her smaller, softer one. His erection pressed into her belly as he kissed her with loving intensity. He smelled of soap from his shower along with his own masculine scent that drew her even closer to him.

He moved his lips from hers and started pressing kisses to her eyelids, her forehead, her cheeks. His lips were so soft against her skin, his touches so special that it brought tears to her eyes. It was as if she could feel his emotions through his fingertips.

"Why are you crying?" He kissed a tear from the corner of her eye.

"I—" She swallowed. "I could have lost you tonight."

"I'm here, sweetheart." He brushed her lips with his thumb. "I'm not going anywhere." He kissed her again before skimming his lips down her neck to the hollow of her throat. "I want to be with you, be inside you, love you."

His words touched her soul. "Yes." She slid her fingers into his silky hair as he moved his mouth over her body. He slid one of her nipples into his mouth and sucked. "Now, Cody," she said on a moan.

She arched her back at the incredible feeling of his mouth on her and was barely aware of clenching her fists in his hair. He ran his tongue over her opposite nipple, teasing it and making it even harder. The ache between her thighs grew stronger yet and she squirmed with desire beneath him. Her need for him was so great it shocked her to her core.

He eased down her body, trailing his lips from her nipples to the valley between her breasts then kissed his way to her bellybutton. He dipped his tongue inside and it caused a thrill to shoot straight between her thighs.

Her skin warmed as he splayed his big hands on her belly while he moved further down and nuzzled her curls. He inhaled deeply, audibly drawing in her scent. He slowly pressed kisses to her mound and to the insides of her thighs and knees. His lips were firm as he trailed his mouth down to her calves and on to her ankles. It was the most erotic thing she'd ever experienced.

He eased back up, pressing his lips to her skin until he reached her mound again. He slipped two fingers into her wet core and she gave a soft moan. It turned into a gasp as he spread her sex open with his fingers and then swiped his tongue up the length of her folds.

Her body vibrated as she arched her back. He licked her with long, slow swipes of his tongue that sent waves of pleasure throughout her. He took his time pleasuring her and when she came she shuddered with the white-hot fire that traveled throughout her from head to toe. Her world spiraled up and up and up until she couldn't form a coherent thought. Every sensation she felt was so powerful.

He rose up, moving his hips between her thighs. He positioned his cock at her entrance then braced his hands to either side of her shoulders as he looked down at her.

"I love you," he said as his gaze held hers. He slid inside her… filling her…stretching her…becoming a part of her.

Her eyes widened as she felt him as if he'd slid inside her, body and soul. He moved in and out in at a slow, deliberate pace.

The way he watched her as he took her made tears come to her eyes. It was so beautiful that her heart squeezed and her thoughts spun. It was all too complicated to work through and right now all she wanted to do was be with him. She didn't want to admit it to herself, but she wanted to always be with him.

Not possible, went through her mind, but she forced the thought aside.

Her lips parted with pleasure as she linked her arms around his neck and didn't take her eyes from his as he continued to move in and out of her.

In moments another orgasm was building inside her, drawing her closer and closer to the edge. Her skin heated, perspiration coating her skin. His body was slick against hers and a droplet of sweat rolled down the side of his face. He looked like it was taking all of his control to hold off his own orgasm.

Fire exploded through her, lighting her mind and body from within. It was like she'd become a furnace inside, her body heated so much that she felt as though she was melting.

Colors and lights spun through her mind and a cry tore from her. He put his mouth over hers, gently holding in her scream.

More sweat rolled down the side of his face and he gritted his teeth, his jaw taut, as his brown eyes held hers.

And then his eyes nearly rolled back in his head as he climaxed. He bit back a shout and it came out as a throaty growl. He thrust in and out as his cock throbbed inside her core.

He came to a stop and braced both hands on the mattress to either side of her head, his strong arms trembling as he held himself over her as if trying to control his body. He lowered his head and kissed her before pressing his lips to her forehead.

Her lips parted as she looked up at him. He'd just given himself to her, had made love to her mind and body and hadn't asked her for anything in return.

He brought her into the circle of his arms, cradling her to him, and tucked her head under his chin. She breathed him in, his masculine scent filling her deeply, his love warming her soul.

She loved him, she knew she did. Why couldn't she tell him?

Too much had happened and was happening. The arsonist… the fact she lived so far away. She couldn't just up and move—

She shut her mind down. Now was not the time to be thinking about things that she couldn't make decisions on in this very moment. She had to think everything through. She didn't know exactly what it was she had to think through, but it wasn't anything she could just make a snap decision on when Cody had just told her he loved her.

And the fact that she knew she loved him, too.

"Penny for your thoughts?" he murmured against the top of her head.

"Buck-fifty," she murmured. "Inflation, of course."

He gave a slow laugh. "You're worth every cent, no matter what you charge."

"I was just thinking what a wonderful man you are." She snuggled closer to him as he slowly stroked her shoulder. "I'm lucky to know you."

"You're a special woman, Carilyn." He wrapped his arms around her. "Just know that I don't intend to let you go."

She said nothing as she rested her head against his chest. She didn't know what today might bring, or each day after that, but for now she would enjoy the moment and her time with Cody.

CHAPTER 20

Nathan sat at his kitchen table, a pile of spent matchsticks on a stainless steel tray in front of him. He struck another wooden matchstick, and watched it flicker before his eyes. The flame burned bright as it began to creep down the stick, closer and closer to his fingers. Mesmerized by the beauty of it, he could barely breathe.

The match's flame flickered and he could see the explosion as if he were right there at that very moment. In his mind he could hear the deafening *boom* followed by the fire's roar.

The explosion had been spectacular. The way it continued to replay through his mind it was like it had just happened rather than having been almost twenty-four hours ago.

After planting the bomb and the Barbie, he'd watched from the bushes, a good distance away. He'd held his breath as everything went up, the flames reaching high into the night sky like white-hot fingers. It had been a living thing of beauty, of true artistry.

Nathan felt heat and then pain as his fingers burned and he dropped the match to the linoleum floor. He stepped on the flame, putting it out, picked up the remnants of the matchstick, then tossed it onto the pile on the tray.

He lit another match, stared into the flame, and his mind turned back to last night.

When the explosion had illuminated the night, he'd cursed as he'd seen a man running away from the house. Nathan had watched the man drop to the ground and moments later Carilyn jumped out of the truck and ran straight to him. It had to be Cody McBride.

In that moment, Nathan could only hope that whatever McBride had been hit with from the explosion had killed him.

Obviously, McBride had found the device before the bomb had gone off. Nathan cursed again. He wasn't an experienced bomb-maker, but he'd done a magnificent job on his first one. It would have been perfect if the timer had gone off when McBride had been inside.

His hope that McBride had been killed faded as he had watched the paramedics attend to the bastard. Nathan had ground his teeth as he'd watched.

Again Nathan's fingers burned and he sucked in his breath as he dropped what was left of the match and stepped on the flame to put it out. He reached down and plucked the stick up from the floor and then tossed it onto the growing pile on the tray.

Fingers red and irritated from being burned, he lit another match and held it up to stare into the flame as he tried to plan his next move.

McBride was weakened now. Nathan had to strike again, and he had to strike quickly and ruthlessly.

The questions were where, when, and how. It needed to be as soon as possible. He smiled to himself. Maybe he should blow up the hotel where McBride and Carilyn were staying. He'd planted a tracking device on the car Carilyn had driven to the ranch, just in case, and now he was glad he had. Early this morning he had tracked them to the hotel they were staying in. He'd retreated to his home base to think…and plan…and think…and plan…

This time Nathan blew out the match before it could burn his sore fingers and he set the stick on top of the pile on the tray. He reached for the matchbox, saw that it was empty, and set it aside.

He reached for a redheaded Barbie sitting on the table to his right. This morning he'd made a run to Phoenix and had gone to three different toy stores to buy redheaded dolls. He hadn't wanted to buy them all at the same place—that might attract attention. And he definitely wouldn't buy anything locally or even as close as Flagstaff.

Of course he'd disguised himself so that if anyone looked at security tapes they wouldn't recognize him. He'd worn a felt hat that he'd pulled low over his eyes, a bushy reddish-brown mustache that matched his beard, and a pair of horn-rimmed glasses. The last thing he'd ever wear was a tweed suit, so that was exactly what he'd worn to the stores when he'd purchased the dolls. His disguise had been perfect.

Using scissors to cut away the packaging, he took the Barbie out of her box then knocked the garbage aside. The doll was wearing a short green dress dotted with big white polka dots, green plastic heels, and had a small green plastic purse. Her red hair was pulled back into a long ponytail and she wore green plastic sunglasses. And of course the requisite big plastic smile.

After he set the Barbie down on the tabletop, he picked up a small can of lighter fluid, which he poured over the pile of matchsticks on the stainless steel tray. He placed the doll onto the pile of matchsticks and poured lighter fluid on her, too.

Earlier he'd set up the laptop, the camera, and the lights. He moved them into place, putting a spotlight on the Barbie and bringing the camera in tight on the doll and the matchsticks. He glanced at his laptop and saw that everything was almost perfectly set up. A few more adjustments and he was ready.

His heart beat faster and he felt a giddy excitement bubbling up inside of him. He grabbed the matchbox and scowled when he saw that it was empty. He got up and dug in a duffel filled with matchboxes and pulled out a large one.

When he sat, he placed the box of matches in front of him then took out a match. He struck it on the side of the box.

Instantly the flame burst on the end of the matchstick. Manic glee overtook him and he almost forgot to click the key on his laptop that would start the recording. The flame was getting dangerously close to his fingers as he started the camera.

It was the first time he'd tried this and he couldn't wait to watch.

He glanced at the laptop and saw the red *record* light was on. With a smile he tossed the match onto the Barbie and pile of matchsticks on the tray.

Fire whooshed up, instantly engulfing the matchsticks and the doll.

He leaned back in the chair and watched as the doll bubbled and burned in the fire. The air was filled with an acrid, bitter odor of burning plastic. He kept the camera going until the fire finally died away.

How he hated to see a fire snuffed out. He loved being able to watch it to the very end of its life. Unfortunately, firefighters put out most fires he set before they could burn all the way down. It was immensely satisfying to be able to watch it all the way to the end.

When the fire was gone, he pressed the key that would stop the recording. He spent the next several minutes watching the video again. When it ended he typed in a message that he made into an image that he tacked on to the end of the video.

A grin spread over his face as he uploaded the video to YouTube, using an account he had named "Firebug" when he'd uploaded another video. He labeled this video, *"You're next, redhead."*

When he was finished, he opened his email account and started a new email.

CHAPTER 21

Carilyn took a drink of ice water then set the glass down while she sat at the writing desk in the hotel and booted up her fourth laptop in just over a week. This time she wasn't bothering with setting up her machine beyond what she had to do to get up and running. Later she would worry about having it the way she wanted for work and personal use.

This time she had one purpose, and one purpose only.

To find the bastard who tried to kill Cody and me.

It had barely been thirty-six hours since the explosion but it felt like it had just happened. She could still hear the massive blast and could still see Cody dropping to the ground.

The thought of him almost dying from the arsonist's bomb made her blood boil in ways it never had before. It had been bad enough that the arsonist had burned up her car. Now he'd blown up Cody's house and had almost killed him and her, too.

The bastard wasn't going to get away with it. She was going to stop him before anyone got seriously hurt or killed. Finding the arsonist had just become her one and only mission.

Yesterday, after getting her new laptop, she'd sent an email to LordoftheFuneralPyre, but she hadn't received a response from him yet. First thing she did after she booted up her laptop was open her email from a web-based browser.

Two emails jumped out at her at once. The first was from *LordoftheFuneralPyre*.

The second was from *Firebug*.

Her throat worked as she stared at the two emails, then made up her mind. She'd open Lord's first, download the software she needed, and track Firebug as soon as she read his email.

She clicked on Lord's email reply.

> *WizardAsp*
> *Getting the feeling you could use a*
> *little luck. This will lead you in the*
> *right direction.*
> *May the force be with you.*
> *LOTFP*

A link was embedded in the email. First she replied to Lord with a brief thank you note, then clicked on the link. The link took her to a secure site where she used her personal passcode and downloaded all of the software she needed. That included the tracking software as well as incredibly sophisticated anti-spyware not available to anyone but the elite hackers who had developed it. She had been one of the developers, so she knew it backward and forward.

The whole time she worked to get what she needed, she continued to think about the email from Firebug, wondering what it said this time.

Someone pounded on the hotel room door and Carilyn startled, knocking the glass of water over. Cold fear iced her veins. Could it be Firebug?

As she stared at the door, she automatically picked up the laptop as water spilled onto the desk's surface.

Ignoring the water pooling on the desk, she got up from her seat, still holding the laptop. A knock sounded at the door again and she flinched.

She set the laptop on the bed and slowly walked to the door. Her heart pounded like mad as she looked through the peephole.

Relief flooded through her followed by shock when she saw who was there.

She opened the door, her eyes wide. "Sam?"

"Hi, baby." He grinned at her. "Surprise."

She stumbled over her words. "How—what are you doing here?"

His blue eyes glinted with amusement. "May I come in?"

"Oh." She brushed her hands down the blouse and jeans she had purchased yesterday before the laptop. She opened the door and stepped out of the way. "How did you find me?"

"Don't I get a hug hello?" He was still grinning. He was five-ten with a runner's physique. He had frequently run marathons before going into the Peace Corps.

"Of course." She let him take her in his arms and hugged him back. "It's good to see you, Sam."

When they parted, he held her by the shoulders and looked her. His grin faded into a frown. "Something's wrong. What is it, Cari?"

She didn't want to explain why she was on edge. She didn't need to worry him, too.

"I'm okay." She tried for a smile but couldn't make it. "What are you doing? How did you find me? Aren't you supposed to be in the Peace Corps for a while?"

"Remember that Find My iPhone application that we installed back when we were dating?" he asked. "It led me right to you. As far as the Peace Corps, I signed up for a short-term technical assignment to get my feet wet. If I liked it I was going to sign up for a long-term assignment."

She felt a stab of irritation that he'd tracked her down using a phone app they'd installed when they were dating. "You should have called."

"I did. Twice." He had the same perpetual air of cheerfulness as he almost always had. "I had to see you."

She tried not to frown. "Why?"

He cupped her face in his hands. "I came back for you. I can't bear to be parted from you any longer."

She stared at him in shock. He caught her completely off guard as he brought her to him and pressed his mouth against hers. She tried to pull away, but he was so strong. She put her hands on his chest and pushed.

He stepped back, still holding her arms. "You haven't forgiven me for leaving you."

"That's not it." She held his gaze. "Let's sit down."

She stepped away from him and sat on one end of the mattress of the king-sized bed with its tangled sheets and bedspread. He sat several inches from her and they faced each other.

She reached out and took his hands in hers. "I've found someone else."

He stared at her in astonishment, no longer looking happy. "You're with another man?"

She gave a slow nod. "I met someone here, in Prescott."

His forehead wrinkled as he frowned. "You haven't been here very long, have you?"

"No." She shook her head. "Not long at all."

"Then how do you know it's real?" Sam gripped her hands. "What you and I had—we were together a long time and you know it was real. We were so good together."

She tilted her head to the side. "You left me. I was hurt, but I got over it."

"Did you really?" he asked as if he didn't believe her. "What we had was special."

She tried to remove her hand from his but he had a firm grip on it. "Yes, it was special," she said quietly. "But you left, and I moved on."

"Give me another chance." He gave her a pleading look. "It can be good again."

"I told you, Sam." This time she was able to extract her hand. "I'm in love with someone else."

He got to his feet, took both of her hands and pulled her to her feet. He gave her a hug. "I'll always be here for you, Cari. If he hurts you in any way, I want you to call me."

"Cody's not going to hurt me." She thought about the fact that she was supposed to be going back to Kansas City in just a couple of weeks—if anyone was going to do the hurting, it would be her. Right now she felt like she was being torn in two.

She pushed all of those thoughts aside. She wasn't going to worry about any of it for now. She smiled. "Thank you, but I'm going to be all right. I'm a big girl."

Sam brought her into his embrace again. "I've missed you, Cari. I wish I would never have let you go."

She let him hold her for a moment, breathing in his familiar scent and feeling his comfortable embrace. She wondered if she did love him still but as she thought about him leaving and going back to Kansas, she felt nothing but fondness for him.

A click and the sound of the door opening had her pushing Sam away. She jerked her attention to the doorway to see Cody standing there, staring at her and Sam.

The look on Cody's face was one of betrayal and anger.

"Cody." Carilyn stepped out of Sam's grasp. "This is not what it seems."

"Is that him?" Sam asked.

Carilyn rounded on Sam. "This is Cody." She turned to Cody. "Meet Sam. I've told you about him."

Cody's expression was hard. "Your ex-boyfriend. Or at least I thought he was your ex."

"He still is." She stepped away from Sam and went to Cody. "Sam tracked me down using the Find My iPhone app we installed back when we were dating. He surprised me."

Cody's eyes were narrowed. "Looks like that was quite the welcome."

"For Heaven's sake." Carilyn put her hands on her hips. "He was giving me a goodbye hug."

Sam walked to where Cody stood and held out his hand. "I'm Sam Anthony."

"Cody McBride." Cody took Sam's hand and the two men looked like they were going to start arm wrestling.

Carilyn swiped loose strands of hair from her face that had escaped her French braid. "Please, let's talk this out."

The men nodded to each other and released their grips.

Sam smiled, but it didn't reach his eyes. "I'm sorry I dropped in on you like this, Cari. I now know that wasn't a good idea."

"It's been good to see you." Carilyn held out her hand and Sam took it. "Give me a call later. Maybe we can all go out for dinner."

Sam released her hand and his gaze flicked to Cody and back to Carilyn. "I doubt if that's a good idea. I have a hotel room at the Best Western. I'll head back there and see if I can get an early flight to Kansas tomorrow."

Carilyn couldn't help but feel bad that Sam had come all the way here to find she was in love with someone else. "Have a good trip back," she said softly. "Keep in touch."

"I will," he said, but the look on his face told her she wasn't likely to be hearing from him for some time, if ever again.

"Bye, Sam," she said as he opened the door.

He gave one look at her, nodded, and closed the door behind him.

The room was silent as he turned to face Cody. He was studying her. "Something is wrong," he said.

She frowned. "I already explained the situation with Sam."

"I'm not talking about that." He shook his head. "There's something bothering you."

"Oh. You're right." She walked to the bed and picked up her laptop. "I got another email from Firebug."

They sat on the edge of the mattress as she opened her laptop, put in her password,

Her heart was pounding as she pulled up her inbox again. She moved her cursor over the sender's name and clicked on *Firebug*. She held her breath as they read it.

> *Sweet Carilyn,*
> *A special video just for you.*
> *Your admirer,*
> *Firebug*

Heat flushed over her at the way he'd called her sweet and had labeled himself an admirer. *Bastard.* She glanced at Cody and his eyes were narrowed.

The embedded URL was a YouTube link. "Let me verify the link does in fact go to YouTube," she said. After she confirmed it, she pulled up the video.

Cold replaced the heat that had burned through her when she saw the title of the video.

You're next, redhead.

Cody clenched his hands into fists.

The user who'd uploaded it was named *Firebug*, and it was one of two videos he'd uploaded.

Her hand trembled as she moved the cursor over the play button.

The video was crisp and clear of a Barbie doll sitting on a pile that looked like burnt matchsticks. A flaming match was lowered by a hand with stubby fingers and then dropped onto the little pieces of wood.

Fire whooshed up, encompassing the Barbie. Carilyn stared in horror as the blaze consumed the doll and bile rose up in her throat. As hard as she tried, she couldn't look away as the flames melted the Barbie, contorting its features, destroying it, and she fought the urge to throw up.

She didn't know how long she watched but finally the fire died out and a message appeared in place of the ruined mess.

"That sonofabitch." Cody's tone was hard, his words a growl as he watched. "I need to call Reese."

Then on the screen words appeared.

You too will burn, sweet Carilyn Thompson. You will burn.

Her stomach clenched and again she almost retched.

Cody's expression was one of fury. He hit the play button, studying the video a second time. Carilyn looked away.

"Here. Look at this." Cody pointed to the screen. "See the ring he's wearing?"

She squinted at the screen. "A blue stone and two snakes." She glanced at Cody. "It looks very unusual."

"I'm going to go after that bastard and make him wish the police had locked him up."

"You need to leave that to the police." Carilyn suddenly felt fear inside her that Cody might confront Firebug. "It's too dangerous to go after him yourself."

Cody didn't respond, but his scowl had deepened as he pulled his cell phone out of its holster. He hesitated as he looked at the screen again. "There's another video uploaded under the same user name."

Her heart set to pounding again as Cody took the laptop from her and pulled up another video. He pressed play and then they saw an image of a woman gagged and bound to a support beam. A Barbie doll with blonde hair was positioned beside her.

"My God," Cody said in a rough voice. "That's Janice Barnhart."

Skin prickling, Carilyn wanted to ask who Janice was, but instead a scream almost tore from Carilyn's throat when she saw the woman suddenly engulfed in flame and crying out behind her gag for help. Carilyn clapped a hand over her mouth to keep from screaming.

"Don't watch." Cody closed the lid of the laptop.

But it was too late. Carilyn continued to see the image of the woman burning, could hear her muffled screams. The scene was burned into her brain and tears rolled down her cheeks.

"Was that real?" she asked in a hoarse whisper.

"I'm afraid it was." He put an arm around her and held her close. "I'm sorry you had to see that."

She clenched her eyes shut but opened them again when the scene played even more vividly behind her eyelids. She felt panic rise inside her like a flock of birds. What if Firebug did come after her? What if he set her on fire, too?

Cody pressed a speed dial number on his phone and put it to his ear. "Reese," he said a moment later. "Are you near a computer? It's urgent."

For a few seconds Cody listened, then said, "Go to YouTube and type in this phrase." He paused, clearly waiting for Reese. "Okay. The phrase is 'You're next, redhead.'"

A moment later, Reese's voice was so loud with anger that she heard him say, "Sonofabitch." He sounded like he wanted to punch something. "How did you get this link?"

"Carilyn got another email." Cody's voice was hard. "But that's not all." Cody looked at Carilyn as he said, "There's another video uploaded by the same user who calls himself Firebug." Cody waited a moment. "Got it? Good."

A minute's pause and then Carilyn heard Reese curse even louder.

Cody listened. "I'll meet you there." He disconnected the call then punched in an address on his cell phone's map application. He faced Carilyn. "I'm going to meet Reese. He has an idea where the second video was shot."

She put her hand on Cody's arm, trying not to show the panic that had her on edge. "Be careful."

"I will." He looked at her. "Stay in the hotel room, okay?"

"I'm not going anywhere." She had an arsonist to track.

They both stood from where they'd been sitting on the bed and she left her laptop on the mattress.

He gave her a big hug. "Everything's going to be okay," he murmured before giving her a gentle. He walked out of the hotel room, closing the door behind him.

Chapter 22

Cody had to force himself to slow down as he drove to the address outside of town that Reese had given him. His rage had been multiplying with every additional thing that happened with the arsonist.

The warehouse was fifteen minutes from the hotel he and Carilyn were staying in. When he reached the warehouse, he recognized Reese's unmarked vehicle along with a police cruiser. Cody parked off to the side and walked into the open warehouse door. Reese met Cody at the entrance as he walked in.

"I've got backup on the way." Reese nodded to a corner of the warehouse where his partner, Detective Kelley Petrova, was examining the scene with two uniformed officers. "There's evidence that something was burned in here recently." He looked like he had to control his expression. "If the video is as real as we think it is, that bastard is a real sicko."

Two more police cruisers and another car pulled up as they were talking. Reese said, "Wait here."

While Reese spoke with the officers, Cody stepped further into the dim warehouse. He caught a charred sickly sweet odor that could only be the remnants of the stench of burnt flesh.

In moments, Reese returned to where Cody waited and the newly arrived police officers started working over the scene. They walked to where two forensics guys were examining the floor. The petite and pretty Detective Petrova stood close by.

Reese started to speak when something metal banged hard on the concrete floor, the harsh sound echoing through the warehouse. Both Cody and Reese looked to see one officer with a crowbar beside a fifty-gallon drum and another with a flashlight pointed down as he looked into a barrel. He drew back, coughing, looking like he was ready to puke, but managed to hold back. Cody recognized the officer as his cousin and Reese's brother, John.

"Reese." John motioned Reese and Petrova to come to him. "I think there's a body here, wrapped in a tarp. It sure as hell smells like it."

John nodded to two officers who pulled the tarp-covered object out of the drum and placed it on the concrete floor. When the officers had untied the rope, they let the tarp fall open.

"Looks like we found the victim," John said. "Or what's left of her."

Detective Petrova, Reese, and Cody looked at the body. The stench was so powerful that Cody's stomach convulsed and he came close to vomiting. Seeing the body—burnt beyond recognition—didn't help. If he hadn't seen the video earlier, he might have lost his lunch.

"Call the M.E.," Reese said.

John had his radio out. "Already on it."

A hard cold rage swelled up inside Cody. "That's probably her."

"We won't know until DNA tests come back." Reese and Cody walked away from the barrel as Reese spoke. "But I have a feeling you're right."

Cody was glad to get away from the body. The last time he had seen Janice Barnhart he'd thought she was a pretty, vivacious blonde. Despite having lost her business to the arsonist, she'd had a surprisingly positive attitude. Seeing her being burned alive on the video not only made him furious, but it made him feel ill. What kind of sick fuck did this to women?

Even though Carilyn was tucked away safely in the hotel room, Cody couldn't help but feel like he should be at the hotel with her. An urgency rose up inside him that he couldn't explain. He needed to get back, and he needed to go now.

* * * * *

When Cody left, Carilyn took a towel out of the bathroom, mopped up the water on the desk, then set her laptop onto its surface.

All that had happened kept churning through her, making her nauseated. The explosion, Sam showing up, Firebug's email, the two videos, and Cody off at some location that could be a trap for all she knew.

She couldn't stop images from pounding in her mind so much so that her head ached with it all.

It didn't do any good worrying about things. What would be productive would be to track down Firebug. She signed onto her laptop and copied Firebug's email address without re-reading the email then minimized the windows for her email and Internet so that she didn't have to see Firebug's name and the video. She would have exited out of the email client and the web browser, but she wanted them to be handy for Cody if he needed them. His own iPad and computer had been lost in the explosion, so he'd had to purchase them new again. He hadn't had time to set-up either of his electronic devices.

She brought up the tracking program she had downloaded earlier and entered Firebug's email address. She took a deep breath and clicked on "start."

For a long moment she stared at the screen, watching its progress but knowing it would take some time to track him down. He was good, really good.

She frowned as she considered that. Was Firebug a computer expert? A hacker even? He had to have some kind of day job, didn't he? She drummed her fingers on the desktop as she contemplated her thoughts.

Feeling suddenly jittery and unable to sit still, she got up from her seat and started pacing the room. She wanted to get out, to go for a walk, to do *something* rather than just sitting here and waiting.

Cody had told her to wait in the hotel room, but what would it hurt to go down to the lobby? She could stretch her legs and go into their coffee shop. She could use a bite to eat, and something with caffeine would be nice, too.

She checked the progress of the tracking program, which was still working, chipping away at every roadblock it came to.

After she stuffed her iPhone in her pocket and cash from her purse in her opposite pocket, along with the keycard, she headed out of the hotel room and to the elevator. It felt good to be moving, good to be away from the computer and thinking about Firebug and the horrible videos. It was as if putting distance between her and her laptop was putting distance between her and Firebug.

Well, at least she was going to try not to think about it all. Her stomach churned as the image of the woman on fire popped into her mind and she pressed her palm to her abdomen. She had to get those images out of her mind. Maybe that hadn't really been a woman on fire. It could be special effects, couldn't it?

She took the elevator down to the lobby, trying to think about anything but the videos and the woman. When the doors parted, she headed out and across the lobby to the coffee shop. The smell of dark roast invigorated her as she went to the counter.

The perky young brunette barista, with *Dahlia* on her nametag, smiled at Carilyn. "Ready for a cup of hot coffee and a pastry?" She inclined her head toward the pastry case.

"Sounds terrific." Carilyn relaxed and looked over the pastries. "I'll have a large dark roast and one of those cheese Danishes." She paid with the cash she'd brought with her then stuffed the change back in her pocket.

Dahlia used a pair of tongs to put a Danish into a small pastry bag and then poured a cup of coffee before giving both to Carilyn. After adding sugar and half-and-half, she sat at a small table near the entrance.

Instead of dwelling on the horrors, she thought about Cody. The way his eyes lit up when he smiled, his sexy little grin, and his hard, muscular body that felt so good against hers when they made love.

Love. Cody had told her that he loved her, but she hadn't been able to say it back to him. It was too soon and she had to think about her life back in Kansas.

As she ate her Danish, her thoughts turned to Sam showing up and how he'd told her he wanted to get back together with her. It had been such a shock to see him, and an even bigger shock to find out why he'd returned.

Could she ever go back with Sam if she returned to Kansas City and left everything she'd come to love here in Prescott? She frowned as she considered it. No, she couldn't. Heck, she couldn't even get herself to think about leaving Cody behind. Just the thought of being separated from him tore her up inside.

She knew the truth. She was in love with Cody and she would do anything to be with him. Including moving to Arizona. She bit into her cheese Danish, feeling a sense of excitement that she hadn't felt before.

Compared to her love with Cody, it seemed to her that her love for Sam had been more friendship than anything.

"Hi." A man's voice jerked her from her thoughts and her eyes shot up to see a vaguely familiar geeky-looking guy wearing a tweed suit. He had stringy hair hanging out from beneath a felt hat, a bushy red mustache, and a beard. He stood over her and was smiling. "Can I sit here?"

The coffee shop had plenty of empty tables and she tried not to frown as she set her Danish on a paper napkin on the table. She really didn't want company right now unless it was Cody.

Before she could respond, the stocky man was pulling out a chair at her table. "Thanks," he said with a smile. "You don't remember me, do you?"

She shook her head as she looked at his longish hair that fell over his bearded face. His smile didn't reach his pale blue eyes behind his horn-rimmed glasses and something tingled at the base of her neck.

"You do seem familiar." She forced a smile. "Where have we met before?"

"At Jo-Jo's." He looked a little put off by her not remembering exactly who he was. "I bumped into you by the bathrooms."

"Oh." Yes, she could see the resemblance although she didn't remember the mustache and he hadn't worn a hat or suit. "I'm sorry. I guess I'd had one mojito too many."

"I'm Nathan." He pushed hair out of his eyes with one hand. She noticed his other hand was below the table. "Why don't we go out for lunch and I'll treat?"

"I can't." She offered Nathan a smile even though she didn't feel like smiling. "I'm waiting for my—my boyfriend to get back."

"Isn't he gone, Carilyn?" Nathan said as he stared at her.

"Cody will be back—" She froze. "I didn't tell you my name."

A grin spread across Nathan's face as he put both hands on the table. Something small and black was in one of his stubby-fingered hands and he wore a silver ring with a blue stone. "I know a lot about you, Carilyn Thompson."

Chills rolled over her body, her scalp prickling. "I need to go. Cody will be here any minute now."

Nathan's expression and his eyes grew cold. "I've been watching you both, Carilyn. I know he just left twenty minutes ago so I'd wager I have a minimum of an hour's head start."

Her gaze dropped to his hand and she looked at his ring again. She grew lightheaded as she realized it was a ring like the one the man in the video had been wearing when he'd tossed a lit match on the pile of matchsticks beneath the redheaded Barbie doll.

"Leave or I'll scream." Her voice shook as she clenched the tabletop with her fingers.

His grin grew more sinister as he opened his hand and laid a small, cheap cell phone on the table. "All I have to do is call a special number and your *boyfriend* will get blown to bits this time."

She stared at him in horror. "Don't. Please."

"It all depends on you." His eyes grew cold. "Come with me now, or I swear I'll bring the wrath of God down on the McBrides and every other cop who's in that warehouse right now."

She didn't have a choice. "Where are you taking me?"

He picked the phone up off the table, pushed his chair back, and stood. "Come on, sweet Carilyn. You'll find out soon enough."

CHAPTER 23

Excellent. Nathan felt almost giddy with excitement as he put his arm around Carilyn's shoulders and walked with her out of the coffee shop. He steered her to the left so that they could head out the back exit.

"Don't give any sign that might make me want to press that speed dial number on the phone," he said close to her ear. "Understand?"

"Yes." She sounded stunned, her voice trembling as she looked straight ahead. "I understand."

They walked down the hall. With his disguise, he was certain he wouldn't be recognized if they ran into anyone. Not that anyone had ever paid him much attention to begin with.

Which was one reason why being Firebug was so much fun. He received plenty of attention now—although anonymously. He knew he'd never be caught. He was too good, too smart. It was almost a shame that no one would ever know he was the genius behind the fires…and Janice's death.

He supposed he'd be considered a serial killer once he took care of Carilyn. He'd have to be even more careful than he already was. The FBI might be called in if they found her body. He wasn't sure that he wanted it to be found, but he did want to make a video and put it up on YouTube, too.

Once he and Carilyn stepped through the rear exit and into the sunshine, he looked around to make sure they were alone. Still keeping his arm around her shoulders, he guided her down the sidewalk to the back of the parking lot. Carilyn slipped in mud at the edge of the sidewalk, the puddle caused by a leaking irrigation bubbler. He scowled as he caught her before she could fall, then jerked her along to a beat-up white Corolla that he'd had for years that he only used for his special "field trips". It was the kind of vehicle that blended in and didn't attract attention.

He opened up the back passenger side door and beckoned to her. She hesitated. He held up the phone and she hurried to slide onto the bench seat. He looked around again then pulled a zip tie out of his tweed jacket pocket.

"Give me your wrists." She did what he told her to and was trembling as he used the zip tie to secure her.

Again he looked around as he took two handkerchiefs out of his other jacket pocket. "Scoot over," he said and seated himself beside her when she obeyed him.

He had her bend down so that she couldn't be seen as he gagged her. Tears rolled down her face and then he put a handkerchief blindfold on her. He worked as quickly as he could, but with his stubby fingers he wasn't exactly deft.

When he finished, he said, "Lie down," then shoved her onto her side.

She gave a muffled groan when her head hit the rear passenger door.

Once again he checked his surroundings as he slid out of the back of the Corolla. He swung her legs onto the bench seat so that her knees were bent and her feet inside the car. He took another zip tie and secured her ankles with it. He picked a blanket up off of the floorboards and spread it over her.

After he was done, he rested his hand on her ass and she shrank away from him. He scowled. He got out and slammed the door shut before going around to the driver's side and climbing in. He locked all four doors, started the vehicle, and backed out of the parking space.

On the way to his destination, he whistled a tuneless tune and grinned to himself. He'd done it again. Just like he'd had Janice Barnhart, he now had Carilyn Thompson.

He drove up into the Bradshaw Mountains for some time until he was deep in the forest and almost to a couple's seasonal home that would be vacant until summer. He'd have to find another place once he was finished with Carilyn.

Or better yet, he could set the cabin on fire with her body inside. It was far enough out of town that he could watch it burn for a long time before anyone showed up to investigate it. He'd have plenty of time to enjoy the fire.

When he reached the cabin, he backed the car up to it then climbed out and opened the back door. He grabbed Carilyn under her armpits and dragged her out of the car. He almost dropped her as her lower half landed on the ground, but managed not to completely let her go.

She didn't fight him as he dragged her out. Clearly she knew it was useless and she didn't want to cause him to trigger the bomb at the warehouse. He did like a fighter, though, so he hoped she'd show a little spirit when he got down to business.

Her legs bumped along the steps when he dragged her up them, and she whimpered. He'd thrown Janice over his shoulder but had ended up hurting his back, so this would have to do. By the time he got her inside the roomy cabin and had pulled her up into a chair he'd set up earlier, he was sweating like racehorse.

Being a redhead, she had a fair complexion, but she looked even paler than he'd noticed before. Not surprising, he supposed, considering that she'd no doubt seen the videos that he'd uploaded. Of course the contrast of the black blindfold and gag against her pale skin was emphasized.

He shrugged off the tweed jacket and tossed it aside, leaving him in a dirty white T-shirt. He raked his fingers through his sweaty hair, and then braced his hands on his wide hips as he stared at her. It was her fault that she was here. If she hadn't rejected him when he'd offered to buy her a drink, if she'd considered going out with him, he would never have had to do what he planned to do now. Like Janice, she deserved it.

He got out a piece of chalk, crouched down and drew a large circle in front of her. That was where he'd pour the gasoline. He wanted to extend the amount of time it would take for the fire to get to her. When he finished drawing the circle, he stood.

What was going on in that pretty little head of hers, he wondered as he walked around her and the chair just outside the circle. He took in her disheveled red hair, wrinkled shirt, dusty jeans, and muddy shoes.

He thought about stripping her out of her clothes and keeping her tied up naked, but decided that would be too distracting. The last thing he needed would be to get distracted when there was so much to do. Besides, he wasn't a rapist and he didn't molest women—rapists were the lowest of the low.

But you're a murderer, Nathan, went through his mind in his mother's voice. *That's as low as you can get.*

"No." He tried to shake off the thought and her shrill tone, but it echoed in his head, over and over again.

You're a murderer, Nathan… Murderer…

He clapped his hands to either side of his head. "Stop it!" he screamed.

Rage tore through him and he stepped forward and slapped Carilyn so hard she fell off the chair. The gag muffled her cry of pain and surprise.

"Bitch." He jerked her up and onto the chair, forcing her back onto the seat hard. He grabbed a rope lying near the camera and then bound her from shoulders to waist to the chair. Her wrists were still zip-tied in back of her, and her ankles were still bound. "It's your fault. Your fucking fault!" he shouted.

With a howl of anger, he jerked off her blindfold. She blinked away the sudden brightness of light in the cabin and stared at him with wide horror-filled green eyes. A red handprint stood out against her pale skin.

As she watched him, he paced the floor, muttering to himself as he kept hearing his mother taunting him. *You're a murderer, Nathan… Murderer…*

With another scream, he dropped to his knees on the floor and clapped his hands over his ears as if that might block the sound of his mother's voice in his head. That old bitch had burned him, left him with a scarred body and mind.

He could feel ropes binding him to a chair and the pain of cigarettes burning into his torso and on the soles of his feet. One time she'd held his hand over a gas flame as he shrieked and sobbed, until his hand blistered. When she was finished, she put burn ointment on the wound and wrapped it with gauze. For a while she left him alone, but then she couldn't help but use him as her personal ashtray.

How he hated her.

But she was his mother. He loved his mother.

He covered his face with his hands and sobbed.

The fury that overtook him was so great that he started shaking with it. He pulled the cell phone out of his pocket and raised it up to show Carilyn.

Her eyes widened with terror and she violently shook her head while crying out at him behind her gag. He watched her as he entered the number to the cell phone at the warehouse and she gave a wordless scream.

CHAPTER 24

The urgency Cody felt was so intense that he couldn't explain it. He had to get to Carilyn. *Had to.*

He started to reach for his cell phone to call Carilyn when something caught his eye on top of a stack of crates. He frowned. It looked like it was probably nothing. But his gut told him to check it out.

Cody jogged to where he thought he saw the unusual object while Reese followed him. Cody went to the pile of old wooden crates. He peered on top of a crate and froze.

A cell phone detonator was strapped to enough C-4 to take out the entire warehouse.

"Clear out!" Cody shouted. "Bomb!"

Reese backed up. "Shit."

Cody and Reese shouted and waved everyone out of the building. Cody's heart pounded harder and harder and his throat went dry.

The moment the place was clear, Reese and Cody ran from the building.

Cody had just made it to the opposite side of a police cruiser, Reese close behind, when the world exploded.

Heat and noise filled the air as the warehouse went up. Reese gave a shout of pain, and when he landed on the ground beside Cody, he was cradling his hand to his belly, blood soaking his white shirt, his face contorted with pain.

"Reese." Cody tore off his T-shirt as fire boiled up into the sky. "Where are you hurt?"

"My hand." Reese grimaced then raised his hand. The last two fingers on his hand had been sheared off. "At least it's my left."

"Damn." Cody wrapped his T-shirt around Reese's hand. "Are you hurt anywhere else?"

"Don't think so." Reese gritted his teeth. "We're going to get that sonofabitch."

"You're damned right we are." Cody squeezed his cousin's shoulder. "Stay here while I check to see if anyone else needs help."

Reese waved him off. "Don't worry about me."

Two police officers were seriously wounded and Reese's partner, Detective Petrova, had been knocked unconscious, but she was coming around. One of the injured officers had taken a piece of shrapnel to his shoulder where it had lodged. Another had a deep cut across his face. A couple of others had minor wounds, but overall they'd made it through relatively unscathed. Thank God he'd taken notice of the bomb.

"Is everyone accounted for?" Reese asked John as he came to stand beside Cody.

John gave a grim nod. "We're all lucky to be here." He focused on Cody. "Thank God you were with us."

Reese clapped his good hand on Cody's shoulder, as the sound of sirens grew louder in the distance. "Thank you," Reese said.

"Damned lucky was it," Cody said, his expression grim. "I need to get back to Carilyn. I've got a bad feeling and I want to make sure she's all right."

"Go on." Reese gave a nod. "I'll catch up with you later."

Still shirtless, Cody turned and hurried to his truck, pulling out his cell phone and dialing Carilyn's number as he ran.

The phone rang several times and the call went to voice mail. He tried again then jammed the phone back into its holster. The drive to the hotel took too long as far as he was concerned. He couldn't get there fast enough. When he arrived, he brought the truck to a hard stop, parking haphazardly near the front entrance of the hotel and bolted inside. Instead of waiting for the elevator, he took the stairs two at a time to the second floor where their room was.

When he reached their room, he pounded on the door with one hand while digging in his pocket for the keycard. "Carilyn, it's me," he shouted. He pulled the keycard out of his pocket and swiped it in the card reader.

A loud click and the door unlocked, and Cody shoved the door open. He didn't see her. He shouted her name and went into the bathroom. She wasn't there. His heart pounded and he tried to calm his breathing. She could have gone down to the coffee shop and he just hadn't seen her as he tore through the lobby.

Her purse and wallet were lying on the bed. He checked her wallet and saw that there wasn't any cash in her wallet. Everything else looked undisturbed.

The new laptop she'd been working on when he'd left was open. He went to it and saw that a program was open and lines of code were rolling by. He wasn't a computer techie so he wasn't sure exactly what it was doing. It was probably the tracking program she'd said she'd be working with.

He'd worry about the program later. Right now he needed to find Carilyn. As he pulled on a clean T-shirt, he dialed her number again. He rushed out of the room and skipped the elevator again. He hurried down the stairs, burst out into the lobby and practically ran to the coffee shop.

A young barista with *Dahlia* on her nametag was at the cash register, and she looked up and smiled as Cody came in. Her smile faded into a look of concern when she saw his expression. "Can I help you?"

Cody went up to the counter. "Did you see a redheaded woman, about five-five, wearing jeans and a T-shirt?"

"Yes." Dahlia didn't hesitate. "She ordered coffee and a cheese Danish, but only took a bite out of the Danish and left her coffee behind when she left."

His heart was pounding hard as he spoke. "Did you see where she went?"

"She left with some weird looking guy," the barista said. "I would never have guessed that she'd be attracted to a man like him, but they walked out with his arm around her shoulders. She didn't look happy. He did have a red mustache, though, so maybe they're related."

Cody tried to calm himself. "What did the man look like?"

Dahlia tilted her head to the side. "I'd say he's around five-nine because he wasn't much taller than me and I'm five-seven. He wore a funny felt hat and a tweed jacket with leather on the elbows, and a white T-shirt under that. I didn't see his eyes."

"Anything else you can think of?" he asked, his whole body vibrating. "Was he wearing a ring?"

"Yeah." She screwed up her face, clearly thinking about it. "I noticed it because the stone was such a pretty blue. It looked like silver snakes or something around the stone."

Cody's blood had gone colder with ever word she spoke. "Did you see which way they went?"

"All I saw was them walking out the door to the left. So they either went to the elevators or out the back exit." Dahlia was frowning. "Is something wrong?"

Cody's body was as tight as piano wire. "How long ago did they leave?"

Dahlia thought about it a moment. "I'd say close to an hour."

Cody bolted out of the coffee shop and headed toward the back exit, pulling his cell phone out of its holster as he ran. He pressed the speed dial number for Reese and held the phone up to his ear. "He's got her," he said as soon as Reese answered.

"What happened?" Reese asked in an urgent tone.

Cody explained all that he knew and gave the man's description as he burst out the back exit into the warm sunlight. He hadn't expected to see anyone, but he'd had to look.

"She left a tracking program running in the hotel room," Cody said. "Maybe one of your computer guys can see if it managed to find the bastard."

"Right away," Reese said, his voice sounding grim. "I'm at the hospital but as soon as they get my fingers, what's left of them, taken care of, I'll be right there. In the meantime I'm sending my guys to the hotel and we'll put out an APB."

After Reese disconnected the call, Cody stood in the back parking lot and dragged his hand down his face. His whole body felt cold and his heart pounded a mile a minute. He turned and headed back into the hotel, back to his and Carilyn's room to look for more clues while he waited for the police.

A sick feeling made his gut feel like it was weighted by a boulder. Firebug had taken Carilyn, the one woman he loved more than anything in this world.

So help him, when Cody got hold of the bastard, he was going to rip him apart. And if anything happened to Carilyn, Firebug was as good as dead.

* * * * *

Carilyn's entire body felt numb as she slouched in the chair against the ropes. Had Cody or anyone else died from the explosion that Firebug had set off? She had no doubt that he had triggered a bomb, no doubt at all.

The rage he had shown, his inhuman screams, had scared her even more than she'd already been. When he'd punched in the phone number for the bomb, her own rage had magnified, but there had been nothing she could do about that but scream behind her gag.

The sound of her phone ringing in her pocket broke the silence and she listened to it helplessly. It had been ringing regularly ever since Firebug had left. She wondered if it were Cody. Prayed it was him, which meant he'd made it and hadn't died in the explosion.

When the phone stopped ringing, she leaned back in the chair, doing her best to swallow the spit that pooled in her mouth behind the gag. Firebug had left through the front what seemed like hours ago. She'd heard the car starting, had heard the crunch of stone beneath tires, and then there was nothing once the sound of the motor had faded. She wondered what he was going to do. Torch the cabin with her in it?

With a shudder, she looked around the cabin yet again. It was a simple place with a great room that was living room, kitchen, and dining area. There were two doors leading from the room—four if you counted the front and rear doors. She assumed the other two led to a bedroom and a bathroom.

On the fireplace mantel was a picture of a large family as well as pictures of children and adults. She wondered if they were related to Firebug, or if he'd picked out a random spot to bring his victims to play with them, or had selected this spot in which to kill her.

In one corner she saw what looked like supplies someone might use to make bombs or something. She'd watched a show on TV where they used lots of C-4 to blow stuff up, and she guessed that's what those clay-like blocks were. There were also wires, a couple of cell phones, and tools, including a pair of pliers, and two duffel bags.

She tried to wriggle in the ropes yet again, hoping for some kind of give, but he had bound her far too tightly. He'd also left the zip ties on her wrists and ankles, and she knew there was no way she'd get out of those. Still she'd squirmed and wriggled, chafing her wrists. Somehow she'd have to convince him to take them off and she was willing to bet there was no chance in hell that he was going to do that.

The sound of an engine met her ears and she perked up. It sounded more like a car than a truck. As it came closer she fantasized that it was someone who could help her. Maybe the owners had returned or somehow Cody had found her. She had to hold out hope.

Rock crunched beneath tires again as the vehicle approached, then the engine was cut and all went quiet. Moments later the front door to the cabin opened and Firebug came in, and her hopes vanished.

He slammed the door behind him with one hand. In his other he had a water bottle that he drank from. The bottle slipped from his hands and bounced on the floor, water spilling over the chalk line he'd drawn. He frowned and picked up the bottle before setting it aside.

The man put his hands on his hips again as he stared at her. The fury he'd exploded with earlier seemed to be gone and he had what might be considered to be a pleasant expression on his face. Pleasant if he wasn't such a sicko and if she didn't hate him so much.

"Comfortable?" he asked almost jovially. He gave a sick smile. "I didn't introduce myself. I'm Nathan. I'm going to have fun with you."

The anxiety crawling up inside her like clawed hands was sky-high. Her stomach turned even queasier than it had been. She tried to focus her oncoming panic attack and turn it into anger. She narrowed her eyes and glared at him. There was nothing else she could do considering she was gagged and bound.

"Sorry to leave you so long, but it was time to visit my mother." He went to her and she fought to keep from shrinking back as he reached for her. She put every bit of hate she felt into her glare. He reached behind her and untied the gag before tossing it on the floor. "She gets upset if I don't visit her regularly."

Her jaws felt sore as she clenched her teeth and looked at him.

"Not so perky now, are you?" he said with an amused look. "I've got you where I want you."

"Let me go." She croaked the words.

His mouth split into a grin. "Yeah, right. And I'll order a limo to take you to your door with a bottle of wine, a box of chocolates, and a dozen red roses while I'm at it."

Her face flushed at his sarcasm and she clenched her hands into fists, wishing she were free so that she could lunge at him and claw his eyes out.

"Oh, let's see." He went to the duffel bags and pulled out a pink box. "Yes, we'll start with this."

Her skin went from hot to cold as she saw that the box was about the same size as one that a Barbie would come in. He busied himself opening the box and eventually pulled out a redheaded doll.

Her heart pounded in her throat as he brought the doll to her and set it on the arm of the chair that she was sitting in, so that it was beside her.

"What are you going to do?" Her voice trembled. She'd asked even though she was sure she knew, but he ignored her question anyway.

"You're just as superficial as this doll, aren't you?" He had a hard edge to his voice and a nasty look on his face. "Too good for someone like me."

She barely heard him as she stared at the doll, horror filling her. In the video with the woman he'd set on fire, there had been a Barbie next to her. Carilyn's stomach churned. Was he going to burn her along with the doll, too?

Nathan returned to the pile of bomb stuff and opened the other duffel. He brought out another box, smaller this time. When he turned to face her, her stomach dropped. It was a box of matches.

He took a match out and struck it on the side of the box. The match burst into flame.

CHAPTER 25

Arnie, the computer forensics tech, examined Carilyn's laptop as Cody talked with Reese in Cody and Carilyn's hotel room. They'd just searched the room for anything that could be a clue to Carilyn's whereabouts, but it looked like all they had was the barista's description and Carilyn's laptop.

Reese's hand was bandaged and spots of blood had appeared where his fingers should be. If he felt pain, he didn't show it. His partner, Detective Petrova, had been ordered to take time off because of the severity of her concussion and the wound to her head. According to Reese, she'd fought with the captain over it, but in the end lost the battle.

"There's got to be some place that we can start." Cody dragged his hand down his stubbled jaws. "The longer it is until we find Carilyn, the greater the chance that we're not going to find her alive."

"We're working on it," Reese said, looking grim.

Cody wanted to tear something apart, anything. He wished Firebug were here so that he could let the bastard have it.

"We've got something." Arnie set a cell phone down on the desk and motioned Cody and Reese over.

Cody's heart rate jumped as he strode to where Arnie sat. "Whatever this program is, it's powerful," Arnie said like an excited kid with a new toy. "Unlike anything I've ever seen. It gave me exactly what I needed."

"Get on with it." Cody couldn't help the gruffness in his voice.

"This Firebug guy hid his tracks so well that it's just amazing that this program got to him," Arnie said.

"Just tell us what you found," Reese said, sounding as impatient as Cody.

"Got his IP address." Arnie handed Reese a piece of paper with a number on it. The name *Nathan Morris* and a Prescott address to a nearby apartment complex were on the paper.

"You got all this from that program?" Reese asked.

Arnie shook his head. "Had to do a little digging of my own and make some calls too, but I'm ninety percent sure this is your man."

"Ninety is good enough for me." Cody started toward the door.

"Good job, Arnie," Reese said over his shoulder as he followed Cody. "Now check out that other ten percent."

Arnie saluted. "You've got it, Detective."

Cody looked at Reese who was grimacing as they headed out the door. "Sure you're okay to go anywhere with the injury to your hand?" Cody asked.

"Think I'm going to let you go after this guy without me?" Reese scowled. "No way in hell." He took out his cell phone and called for backup, giving the suspect's name, the description the barista had given Cody, and the physical address.

Fortunately it was a relatively close apartment complex, so it took little time to reach it. Cody wanted to go straight to the apartment and beat down the door, but Reese held him back until backup had arrived, which included John.

When everything was ready, Reese, Cody, and the officers went to the apartment. Reese banged on the door. "Police. Open up."

No answer. Reese banged on the door and called out again. Still no answer. He nodded to a pair of officers holding a battering ram. It took two attempts to break in the door. Wood splintered and the door swung open, now partially unhinged.

Reese and the officers cleared the small apartment. When they'd confirmed no one was there, Cody joined Reese in looking through the area.

"Sonofabitch." Cody looked at a bank of monitors. One screen had Leigh's house in view and another was on the hotel that Cody and Carilyn were staying in. He recognized the homes of Firebug's other fire victims on screens as well.

"Look at this, Cody." Reese's jaw was set in a firm line as Cody looked at him.

He moved to Reese's side and saw what he was looking at. "Holy shit," Cody said, his gut clenching. It was a scrapbook filled with pictures of the arsonist's victims, their homes or places of businesses on fire, surveillance photos, and newspaper articles. There were multiple surveillance pictures of Carilyn, her burning car, as well as the photo of Carilyn, Leigh, and their friend that had been taken from Leigh's house.

"We found these." John McBride brought in three duffel bags from the bedroom and showed Reese and Cody the contents. One had several boxes with Barbies in it, another contained glass wool tubes, and a third looked like it had enough C-4 to blow up half of Prescott.

They continued to search the place for clues as to where Firebug might have taken Carilyn, but they found nothing.

Cody looked at Reese. "If her cell phone's on, we could track her."

Reese blew out his breath. "With a warrant."

Cody clenched his hands into fists. "We don't have time for that." His mind raced. How could he track her? Then it occurred to him. Carilyn's ex-boyfriend had tracked her using the Find My iPhone app. He just needed to locate him. What was his name? Sam…Sam… "Sam Anthony," Cody said out loud.

"Who?" Reese said with a questioning look.

"I think I know how we can do it," Cody said in a rush. He explained how Carilyn's ex-boyfriend had tracked her down. "I hope to God he's still in town. He said he was staying at the Best Western."

Cody pulled his phone out of its holster and called information. He didn't have time to look it up on the Internet on his phone. He was connected to the hotel right away and he asked for Sam's room.

A man answered on the second ring. "Sam Anthony?" Cody asked.

"Yeah." Sam sounded wary. "Who's this?"

"Cody McBride." His heart was beating faster. "I don't have time to explain but I've got to find Carilyn and I'd like to track her with the app that you found her with. It's an emergency."

"Why?" Sam's voice was instantly filled with concern. "What's going on? What happened to her?"

Cody started walking toward the door and gave a nod for Reese to follow him. "She's missing."

"Missing?" Sam repeated. "Explain."

"I'm on the way to your hotel with the police," Cody said as he and Reese hurried to the stairwell and through the door. "We think she's been kidnapped."

"Oh, my God," Sam said. "I'll meet you outside the front entrance."

"We'll be right there," Cody said and disconnected the call.

Cody and Reese rushed to his car. Reese put on the flashers and siren on his unmarked vehicle and they tore through the streets to the hotel. The Best Western was within minutes of the hotel that Cody and Carilyn were staying in.

Sam was waiting outside like he'd said.

"We'll take your phone," Cody said as he rolled down the window and Sam hurried to the car.

"I'm going with you." Sam jerked open the rear door before Cody could reply.

"Stay in the car when we get there." Reese spun out of the parking lot. Clearly Reese felt they didn't have time to argue. "Give your phone to Cody."

Cody took the phone and examined the location. "Damn. The sonofabitch has her in the Bradshaws."

Sirens going and lights flashing, Reese called for backup as he tore through town toward the mountains.

Cody's gut was churning. They had to find Carilyn. She had to be okay.

For the first time in a long time, Cody prayed.

* * * * *

Carilyn's entire body shook as she watched Nathan light matches. He looked at the flames like a lover watching his mate remove her clothing, until the fire burned down to his fingers. He dropped burnt matchstick after burnt matchstick into a pile on a kitchen table.

Every now and then he would grin at her and she knew he was toying with her, doing his best to frighten her.

It was working.

She was tied up in a cabin, God knew where, and no one knew where she was. She swallowed. Somehow she would have to save herself.

How? She bit the inside of her cheek as she hopelessly strained against her bonds. *How am I going to save myself?* Images of the woman being burned alive were seared into her retinas and she could see it as if she was watching the video now. The flames, the muffled screams behind the gag, the terror...the body...

A tear rolled down Carilyn's cheek and she wished she could wipe it away before he saw it. She didn't want to show weakness in front of this bastard, but she hadn't been able to help herself.

Nathan grinned at her, affirming that he had seen the tear and liked seeing her scared, that he reveled in it. "It won't be long, my sweet Carilyn."

"Don't call me that." She glared at him. "I'm not your anything."

He chuckled. "I'd say you certainly belong to me now." He gestured around them. "Do you see anyone else? There's no one here who cares for you the way I do."

"You pig." A part of her snapped. "You're nothing but a loser who gets off on hurting and killing women."

A clear change went over him and she instantly regretted her outburst. "I'm going to enjoy watching you burn," he said in a nasty tone. With his brows narrowed, he went back to lighting matchsticks.

Eyes watering, she looked at the camera he had set up on a nearby tripod. He'd turned it on just before he'd started lighting matches and it was recording everything…everything but him. He was clearly out of the scope of the lens.

She squeezed her eyes shut tight. Dear God, what was she going to do? Was she going to die here, burned alive by this—this insane man?

"Watch me." Nathan snapped the words. "Watch or I'll light you on fire now."

Carilyn looked at him, a burn in her throat and pressure behind her eyes. She tried to avoid his gaze and instead stared at a crack in the wall just over his left shoulder.

"Look at me, Carilyn." Nathan spoke in a warning tone as she heard the scratch of another match.

She swallowed and met his gaze, and then she shuddered at the death in his eyes. Her death.

"Please let me go." The tears in her voice were impossible to avoid. "Please."

He gave a bitter laugh. "It's your fault, you know."

"How is it my fault?" she managed to ask.

He shrugged as he paused in lighting matches. "If you hadn't rejected me that night at Jo-Jo's, I wouldn't have to do this."

"I was with someone else." A pleading note was in her words. "I couldn't just leave him."

Nathan snorted. "You could have told him you were leaving with someone else."

"I would have hurt his feelings," she said.

"So instead you hurt mine." He sneered. "It's okay to hurt me just because I'm not as good-looking as your boyfriend."

It's because you're a sadistic creep, went through her mind. Instead, she said, "Maybe if I'd met you first—"

"Shut up, bitch." His expression grew darker. "You'll say anything hoping I'll set you free."

She bit the inside of her lip again, biting it hard enough that she tasted blood, just to keep herself from showing any more weakness.

The pile of matchsticks grew and he hummed to himself. He looked extraordinarily pleased as he scratched matchsticks on the box and watching each flame until it died away.

"What could I do to make you happy?" She was grasping at straws. "I'll do anything."

"Shout my name as you die." He gave her a look that told her he was aroused. "I can't wait to hear your screams while I watch you burn."

Feeling sick to her stomach, she stared into the flames as she watched matchstick after matchstick burn, knowing it all would come to an end soon.

When he burned the last matchstick, he scooped them up and set them on the chalk line, close to her feet. Her terror grew as she watched him take gasoline and pour it over the large circle that surrounded her.

He picked up the matchbox. "One match left." He smiled, a sick, satisfied smile. "You'll get to watch the fire burn in a circle around you," he said. "Gradually it will close in until you're on fire, too."

He struck the matchstick and held it over the gasoline-soaked chalk line.

CHAPTER 26

Reese, Cody, and Sam raced against time, finally reaching the foothills of the Bradshaw Mountains. Once Cody had figured out that Carilyn had been taken, he'd stopped calling her phone because Firebug, who he now was certain was Nathan Morris, might hear it and turn it off.

For all Cody knew, Morris could have heard the phone already and planted it someplace to send anyone trying to find her on a wild goose chase. Cody prayed that wasn't the case. He prayed Carilyn was exactly where the phone app said she was.

"Dear God," Sam said in a frantic voice and Cody glanced over his shoulder at him. Sam's face was pale and his teeth were clenched. "Can't you drive any faster?"

The car fishtailed as Cody turned his gaze on Reese who said, "If we go any faster we'll end up in the ditch. I'm doing what I can without losing control on this road."

Sam crossed his arms over his chest and looked out the window. "Why did this guy kidnap Carilyn? I think you should explain it to me."

Cody looked at Reese who gave a slight nod. "Tell him without giving the details we're keeping from the press." Which meant Cody wasn't to tell Sam about the Barbie dolls.

Starting at the beginning, Cody gave Sam the Cliff Notes version of the case and what had been happening to Carilyn. He didn't mention Janice's burnt body or the videos of her being burned alive.

"Dear God," Sam said again when Cody finished telling him the pertinent information.

"We're getting closer to her." Cody glanced at the phone, his heart throbbing painfully in his chest. "The app says we're within five miles."

Reese turned off the siren and lights as they got closer. Backup was four or five miles behind them.

Cody was afraid the phone's app wouldn't get them far in the mountains, just like the mapping app gave them problems once they got to rural areas. However the Find My iPhone app seemed to be more powerful than the mapping application.

When they came to a fork in the road, Cody told Reese to turn left. A little ways further, the app told him they needed to make a right. The phone was within half a mile if the app was correct.

Cody's heart beat faster as they approached. "We should stop here," he said as they came within two hundred feet of the location. They couldn't see anything ahead, but didn't want to be spotted.

"Stay with the car," Reese said to Sam. "I need you to tell my men which way we went. If you follow, I have to I'll cuff you and lock you in. Understand?"

Sam set his jaw but nodded.

Reese and Cody climbed out of the car. "You stay back," Reese said. "I'm breaking the damned rules letting you come with me."

Cody nodded, with no intention of staying back at all.

They headed through the brush, careful to stay out of sight. Finally, up ahead they saw a cabin through the trees. Reese started to step forward when Cody grabbed his arm, stopping Reese. Cody pointed down at a silver wire that glinted in the little bit of sunlight that filtered through the pines.

"A trip wire," Reese said grimly, echoing Cody's thoughts.

Cody nodded. "Looks like it."

While Cody marked a tree, Reese took out his cell phone and called the dispatcher to have her let backup know about the trip wire.

"We'll wait a few minutes 'til a couple of my men get here to show them where the wire is." Reese was holding his mutilated left hand close to his side. The spots of blood were bigger now. "I'll also have backup then."

Cody gritted his teeth, not wanting to wait, but knowing they had to in order to make sure no one tripped the wire. God knew if it would trigger a bomb or something alerting Morris to their presence. He figured Reese was probably missing his partner, Detective Petrova. They were one hell of a team.

It was only a few minutes before two officers, one of whom was John McBride, met up with Reese and Cody.

"Stay here," Reese said to Cody as he stepped over the wire.

Cody ignored him and stepped over it, too. John followed but said nothing.

"Damn it, Cody," Reese muttered. "Just make sure you stay clear. I don't want you getting harmed."

They eased through the brush, closer and closer to the cabin. An older model white Corolla was parked in front of it. When they reached the edge of the brush, Reese and John drew their weapons and made sure it was clear.

"Stay here, Cody," Reese growled. "Wait until I tell you it's safe." He looked at the cabin. "If it's safe."

Cody prayed Morris didn't have any surveillance cameras set up as Reese and John crouched low and made their way to the cabin.

In spite of what Reese had ordered him to do, Cody started to follow—and then he smelled something burning.

His gut clenched as he saw smoke coming through a partially open window.

* * * * *

Nathan laughed as the fire started to burn hotter in a ring around Carilyn, and terror ripped through her. The circle smoked where the water had been spilled on the chalk line he'd put around her and he coughed as the smoke streamed past his face. The smoke made her cough, too.

"I'm going to have to leave soon," he said in between coughs, "but I want to watch you go up in flames."

Tears rolled down her cheeks as she struggled harder against her bonds, knowing it would do no good. She couldn't help the tears, but damn it, she wasn't going to scream. She didn't want to give him the satisfaction.

But as the flames grew higher on the chalk line, the heat becoming oppressive, she couldn't stop herself. She let out a scream of fear so loud that her throat hurt. She was going to be burned alive.

Nathan smiled. "Good, good." He backed away from the fire, a look of rapture on his face. "I like that. Scream again."

Sweat dripped down the sides of her face, as it grew hotter. She clenched her teeth to hold back any more screams, but she knew it was going to be impossible to hold them back once her flesh started to burn.

A crash echoed through the cabin and she startled. Through the flames she saw Nathan whirl around.

"No!" he shouted as he held out his arms as if to keep anyone from passing him. He backed up to the flame. "You can't have her!"

"Hands over your head and get away now or I'll shoot," came a voice she knew and her heart leapt.

"No!" Nathan took another step back.

His clothes caught fire.

He shrieked as he went up in flames. The next thing she knew he'd dropped on the floor and was rolling around.

Through the flames she saw a figure rush forward. In the next moment, Cody was in the circle of fire with her.

"Cody!" Relief flooded her but she felt a burst of fear for him. What if he caught fire?

"Get the bag of C-4 and get the hell out of here," she heard Reese McBride shouting to someone. "There might be more explosives that we can't see. Cody, hurry!"

Cody grabbed her, chair and all over his shoulder. Carilyn screamed as he leapt back through the flames with her.

She felt a flash of intense heat and then he'd set the chair down. His gaze swept over her and she saw that his clothes were on fire. Hers were not. He dropped on the floor and rolled to put out the flames where his T-shirt had started to burn. He surged back to his feet, grabbed her and the chair again, flinging her over his shoulder, and he rushed for the door. Police officers were clearing out of the cabin, too, and one of them had Nathan.

Cody jogged down the porch steps with her and didn't stop running. She saw others tearing away from the flames, too. As they ran through the trees, an explosion came from behind them. Cody stumbled forward and she screamed as they both went down.

They hit the ground hard, knocking the breath from her, the chair bruising her flesh and her head landing on a soft patch of ground. Another explosion ripped through the air and Cody flung himself over her to protect her from any falling debris.

After a moment he got to his knees and reached into his pocket. "Are you hurt anywhere?" he asked as he pulled out a pocketknife.

She stared up at the face that she'd thought she'd never see again. A face so dear to her that she couldn't imagine being away from him ever again. "I don't think so. I feel okay."

He sliced through her bonds, then grabbed her again. "We've got to get out of here. The whole damned forest might go up."

"I can run," she said as he flung her over his shoulder again, this time minus the chair, which he left behind.

He didn't listen to her, as if he didn't want to let go of her. His feet pounded on leaves and rocks as he tore through the brush and trees. It felt like he was running forever.

She heard the roar of fire, along with the crackle, hiss, and popping sounds of the fire burning the forest. She could feel the fire rushing down on them.

From her side vision, she saw Nathan cuffed and being dragged along by his arm, through the forest. Despite the dire circumstances, she felt a rush of satisfaction to see Nathan in custody.

She saw that portions of his clothes were burned off and angry blistered patches of skin were showing through the large holes. She felt no sympathy toward him, none at all.

They burst through the trees to where several cars were parked. All but one of the vehicles were marked police cars.

Cody adjusted her in his arms. Someone had jerked open a car door and he thrust her inside the back seat and climbed in after her. Reese was in the driver's seat and someone else was sitting in the front passenger seat.

Reese started the car, backed up, then turned the car around and shot out onto the road. She saw the police cruisers doing the same thing. When she looked over her shoulder, through the back window she saw that the forest was on fire.

Cody swept her up in his arms and gave her a fierce, hard kiss. "I was so afraid for you," he said and kissed her again.

"Thank God," came another familiar male voice from the front passenger seat. She shot a look at him and saw that it was Sam.

"Sam." She stared at him in surprise. "What are you doing here?"

"The iPhone app." He nodded to Cody. "He got hold of me just as I was getting ready to leave town and we used it to find you."

"Thank you," she said, her eyes filling with tears from the smoke, the fact that she'd almost been burned alive, and because of the men who'd saved her. "Thank you all."

Cody held her tightly to his chest, drawing her into his lap. "I am never letting you go, Carilyn. I love you so damned much."

Vaguely she was aware of Sam watching and the pain in his expression, but she had to tell Cody how she felt.

"I love you, Cody." She met his gaze. "You mean everything to me."

CHAPTER 27

Carilyn took a long drink from a bottle of spring water as she leaned up against a counter in Leigh's kitchen. Leigh was in her room taking a shower.

Will life ever feel normal again? Carilyn wondered. She thought maybe it would now that Leigh was back and they'd scrubbed the house from top to bottom, as if that would eliminate every trace that the home had been ransacked. She was still adjusting after her traumatic experience, but with every day that passed, she felt more and more healed.

Of course when she'd returned, Leigh had been shocked at everything Carilyn had been through and had supported Carilyn in every way possible.

It had been three weeks since she'd almost been murdered. Nathan Morris was still in a burn trauma unit from third degree burns all over his body. Once the hospital released him, Reese, who was back at work as soon as the doctor cleared him, had assured her that Nathan would be sent directly to jail without passing Go. There would be a trial of course, and she'd need to be in Prescott to testify and see him go to prison, but she wasn't going to think about all of that just yet.

"When is Cody getting here?" Leigh asked as she came into the kitchen while pushing her blonde hair behind her ears.

Carilyn looked at the clock on the coffee maker. Her stomach skipped with excitement. "Any time now."

"I can't tell you how thrilled I am that you and Cody are together." Leigh looked absolutely delighted. "I knew you two would hit it off."

The doorbell rang and Leigh smiled. "Looks like your Prince Charming is right on time."

Carilyn gave a quick grin. "He may not be a prince, but he is a rather charming cowboy fireman, I have to say."

Leigh hooked her arm through Carilyn's and they walked through the kitchen and into the living room. "Any idea what Cody has planned for you two this weekend?"

"Nope." Carilyn shook her head. "But my bags are packed just like he told me to, and I included everything he suggested."

"I love surprises." Leigh smiled as she released Carilyn and reached for the door handle. "Mike's an awesome guy but he needs a few lessons in that area."

Leigh opened the door wide and waved Cody in. Carilyn wanted to melt at the sight of him in his Wrangler jeans, cowboy boots, and the Stetson he wore when he wasn't on duty at the fire station.

"Hi, Leigh," he said before he grinned at Carilyn and gave her a wonderful kiss that made her feel light as air.

"Where are you off to?" Leigh asked brightly when Cody and Carilyn parted.

"Good try." Cody winked at Leigh before glancing around her living room. "Your place looks great now that you're back and it's set to rights. I have to say Mike is a lot easier to get along with since you've come home. Especially now that I've been living with him since my house was blown to hell."

Leigh gave a laugh. "I had a wonderful time in Europe, but I'm happy to be back. I missed him, too." She smiled at Carilyn. "And I'm so happy to have you here."

"Ditto on Carilyn being here," Cody said with a look at Carilyn that made butterflies dance in her belly. "As far as Mike is concerned, I've never seen him like this before," Cody added. "I think he's got it for you bad."

Leigh grinned. "I like the sound of that."

Cody looked at Carilyn. "Ready?"

She gestured to her new pink suitcase. "Yep."

He picked up the suitcase. "See you, Leigh." He touched the brim of his hat and nodded to her before turning and heading out the front door.

Carilyn gave Leigh a quick hug. "Have a great time," Leigh said as she drew away.

"Thanks." Carilyn smiled at Leigh and whispered so that Cody couldn't hear. "Maybe you should plan a surprise trip for you and Mike and show him how it's done. Sometimes men need a push."

Leigh looked thoughtful. "Now there's an idea."

Carilyn said goodbye and Leigh watched them as they climbed into Cody's truck. Leigh waved as Cody started the truck and pulled away from the curb. Carilyn waved back.

She turned to Cody. "So where are we going?"

"I'll never tell," he said with a grin and she lightly punched his arm.

They chatted about his new home—the builders would be starting on it soon. Just days ago, Carilyn had surprised Cody with a new guitar that she'd bought him to replace the one that had been lost in the explosion.

As for the explosion itself, and everything else bad that had happened, she appreciated that he didn't bring it all up. She still had nightmares over the bastard who'd nearly killed her. Not a day had gone by since then that thoughts of all that had happened hadn't flitted through her mind. But she was getting better, one day at a time. Time would heal the wounds as the memories faded and became more and more distant. Eventually, anyway.

She glanced out the window as he drove. After a while, her eyes widened. "Oh, my gosh. The red rocks are so beautiful."

He gave a nod. "Yep."

"That's your surprise!" She gave an excited bounce in her seat. "We're going to Sedona."

With a smile he said, "You've guessed right."

"I've been wanting to go since I arrived in Prescott." She looked in wonder at the scenery. "This is absolutely incredible."

He pulled off the road into a scenic outlook. "We'll stop so you can take a look."

Before she could climb out herself, like always he was there to hold the door open for her. She walked up to the overlook and gazed at the gorgeous rock formations and felt the spiritual pull of the place.

"It's amazing." She looked at him and smiled. "Thank you for bringing me here."

After she'd had her fill of the view, at least temporarily, they climbed into the truck and were back on their way. They went through what felt like a dozen roundabouts as they headed through the Village of Oak Creek and into Sedona.

When they drove into the town, she looked in delight at everything around them. Soon he was pulling up to a rustic bed and breakfast nestled amongst juniper and pine trees. Manicured gardens surrounded the place.

"It's beautiful," Carilyn said in a breathless voice as Cody parked. Once he'd helped her out of his truck, he grabbed her small suitcase and his duffel bag and carried them into the B & B's lobby.

Inside there were so many things to look at. Native American artwork decorated the cozy lobby. Cody checked them in and it wasn't long before they were in their own room with a private patio. The room had a king-sized bed and a jetted tub in the large bathroom that was tiled with red stone.

"It's wonderful." She wrapped her arms around his neck after they looked around the room. "You are amazing."

"Get ready, and wear the dress I told you to pack," he said with a smile.

She felt almost giddy as she dressed and touched up her makeup. When they headed out, the day was waning and cool shadow lay over the land.

"It's wonderful here." She breathed deeply of the fresh air and stretched her arms wide. "More than this Kansas girl ever expected." She closed her eyes and let the power of the place soak into her skin, soak into her soul. "I love this place."

She opened her eyes and caught him grinning as he watched her and she grinned back.

They left the B & B and he took her to a lovely restaurant where they were seated in a corner at a table for two and given elegant menus. Cody ordered a bottle of Chardonnay and it arrived before they'd even had a chance to look at their menus.

After pouring each of them a glass, the server set the bottle down and started to light the candle at the middle of the table. Both Cody and Carilyn held out their hands in a stop gesture and said, "No!"

The server looked surprised but gave a slight bow and turned away. Cody and Carilyn looked at each other and laughed.

Carilyn shook her head. "I've had enough fire to last me a lifetime."

The corner of Cody's mouth quirked. "I'd say the same, but my career won't let me get away from it."

She studied him. "I don't think I could go a day without worrying about you every time you went to work."

He reached across the table and put his hand over hers. He rubbed the back of her hand with his thumb in slow circles. "You don't need to worry about me, Carilyn."

"But I do." She looked down at their hands before meeting his gaze again. "After everything, I feel even more like I'd worry every time you'd leave for the fire station." She turned her hand up and they linked fingers. "But at the same time I'm so proud of you for doing something that saves lives. What you do truly matters."

He raised her hand and brushed his lips over the back of it, causing her to give a little shiver.

She studied him before she said, "I booked a flight back to Kansas on Wednesday."

He went still but his hand gripped hers tighter. "You're leaving?"

She nodded. "Yes."

"Carilyn," he said with urgency, "I can't imagine life without you."

With a sly smile, she said, "Well I have to go back. I need to pack up my apartment if I'm going to move to Prescott."

Cody let out his breath in a whoosh and his face split into a grin. "Thank Heaven, because it wouldn't be so easy to sell my property and follow you to Kansas."

Her eyes widened. "You'd do that for me?"

"Hell yes." He took both her hands in his and held them tightly. "I love you so damned much, Carilyn. I don't want to ever live without you. I won't live without you."

"I love you, too, Cody." She gripped his hands just as tightly. "I can't imagine not having you in my life."

When he leaned forward, she met him halfway and they kissed. It was sweet and wonderful, and she couldn't remember ever being so happy in all her life.

He released one of her hands, picked up his glass of wine, and raised it. "Here's to us and a future filled with new possibilities."

She smiled and raised her own glass. "To us," she said softly and clinked her glass against his, excited for the future and everything to come.

Excerpt... Crazy For You

Cheyenne McCray

The afternoon was growing long as she reached a stock tank, not too far from a small thicket of oak and mesquite trees. She dismounted and let Poca drink from the tank.

Ella felt a prickling along her spine and looked around to see a horse and rider approaching. Clint. A strange combination of irritation and pleasure traveled up and down her spine. Irritation that he had followed her, and pleasure that he was there. Then irritation at her pleasure.

Frowning, she turned her attention to Poca, ignoring Clint. Out of the corner of her eye she watched him dismount Charger when they reached the tank and then lead his horse to the water. She noticed a blanket rolled up on the back of Charger's saddle.

She glanced at him. "What are you doing out here?"

"Checking up on you." He said the words casually.

She scowled at him. "What right do you have—?"

In the next moment he gripped her upper arms so tightly that she caught her breath in surprise. The look in his brown eyes caused her heart to pound and she dropped Poca's reins to brace her palms on Clint's chest, ready to push him away.

He had never looked as handsome as he did that moment, his expression so intense that she felt as if she might be consumed by the need she felt emanating from him. A raw, powerful need that she shared with every part of her being.

She swallowed as flutters traveled through her belly. "Let me go, Clint."

His expression turned serious, but he didn't let her go. "I have one question for you. Whether or not I let you go depends on the answer to that question."

She raised an eyebrow. "And that would be?"

"What's your relationship with Johnny Parker?" he said slowly.

Confused by his question, she blinked. "We're good friends. Why?"

"That's all I needed to hear." He dragged her up against him and his mouth came down hard on hers.

Completely caught off guard, she let out a startled gasp, but he swallowed it with his kiss. It was powerful and demanding as he slipped his tongue into her mouth and he gripped her ass in his big hands. His cock was hard as he held her tightly to him.

The thought of struggling came to a quick death as she fell into the kiss. She gave a soft moan as he ground his erection against her belly and she felt an answering tingle between her thighs. Not just a tingle but a full on explosion of need and desire. She thought about the night he had touched her and brought her to orgasm and she gave a soft moan.

She grew lightheaded, as if she needed more oxygen. When he drew away she stared up into his eyes. "I need to finish checking the fence line." The words came out in a husky whisper, as if she wasn't sure about herself, not at all like she'd intended.

"You need to stay right here." He moved his lips to her ear. "With me."

A shiver traveled down her spine. "No." She swallowed. "I need to—"

He took her mouth hard again and she felt every bit of resolve slipping. How many times had she dreamed of his kisses? And now that she was a grown woman, here she was, in his arms.

Her whole body felt like soft clay, as if he could mold her, shape her, make her a work of art with his touches and kisses. He groaned deep and low in his throat and she shivered again as he moved his palms from her ass to her waist and back again. His hands felt sure and strong, and she felt a sense of possessiveness running through him, as if she belonged to no other.

No, he was just trying to change her mind and she couldn't allow him to get away with that.

She shoved at him hard, breaking the kiss, severing the fire that had made her feel connected to him in ways she couldn't have imagined. "That's enough."

"I'm just getting started." He caught her up in his embrace so that his arm was beneath her ass and she was halfway over his shoulder.

She struggled in his arms. "Put me down, Clint." He was so strong that she could barely move.

He held on to her with one arm and with his other he unbuckled two straps holding the rolled up blanket on the back of Charger's saddle.

It occurred to her then exactly what he planned to do with that blanket. She tried to get away but he carried her to the thicket of oak and mesquite trees. He unfurled the blanket on the ground with his free arm, at the base of a group of rocks that were beneath the trees.

He turned and twisted her in the air and she let out a surprised cry as he sat on one of the big rocks. In the next moment she found herself laying facedown, over his knees, her arms pinned behind her back, her hair hanging over her face.

"You deserve a spanking for being so damned difficult," he growled.

A spanking? Hell no. "Let me go, Clint. Or I swear you'll regret it."

"Be still." He held her wrists in one hand then swatted her hard with his other.

The sting caused her to cry out and her eyes watered. "Don't!" Again he swatted her and again she cried out. "Stop it!"

To her shock, she felt a tingling between her thighs as he spanked her. She didn't know how it could be, but with every swat she pictured him thrusting inside her. Her breasts ached and her nipples were hard nubs. She wriggled and felt his rigid cock against her body.

He paused and rubbed her ass with his palm. "Will that make you be quiet and listen?"

"You're a big bully." She realized her breathing had quickened and a thrill had coiled deep in her belly. "I'll never be quiet with that kind of treatment."

"Is that so?" He swatted her again, harder this time, and she felt a greater tingling between her thighs. "I think you like it."

"Never." The more she fought him, the more turned on she was getting.

He moved his fingers between her thighs and she caught her breath. He had to feel her heat and maybe even how damp she was through her jeans.

Her head spun, her hair flying around her face, as he swept her up and held her to him. Automatically she wrapped her arms around his neck and her thighs around his waist and held on.

He laid her on her back on the blanket. She started to scramble away but he grabbed her leg and pulled her to him. She tried to kick free but he was on her, pinning her legs between his thighs and holding her wrists above her head as his big body pressed her to the makeshift bed.

She was pinned so securely that there was no struggling now. Before she could utter another word, he kissed her hard. At first she refused him, but she melted and gave in to the kiss and answered back with the same intensity he showed her.

He kept her arms above her head with one hand and pushed up her T-shirt with his other. She gasped as he moved his mouth to her cloth-covered nipple.

His mouth was hot and wet, his tongue teasing, and he lightly scraped her nipple with his teeth. She gave in completely and barely realized he had let her arms go as he moved his mouth to her other breast.

He rose and tugged her T-shirt up, yanked it over her head, and laid it over the rock he'd been sitting on. He reached beneath her and unfastened her bra and pulled it away from her. The air was cool on her nipples and she felt an amazing sense of wickedness at being bare outside on the range.

After he tossed the bra aside to land on top of the blouse on the rock, he moved over her and braced one hand to the side of her head.

"Are you going to be good?" His expression was dark and intent as he reached between them and unfastened her belt. "You know what I'll do if you aren't."

She swallowed. She could fight him and she knew he'd catch her and punish her all over again. That thought sent another thrill through her and she was tempted to struggle just to be manhandled by him. But at the same time she didn't want to fight him anymore. She wanted whatever he would give her.

He brushed his lips over hers. "Are you going to fight me?"

She shook her head. "No."

His smile was slow and sensual and he eased down her body. He knelt at the foot of the blanket and watched her as he took one of her boots in his hands and slipped it off before setting it aside. He took off the other boot before removing her socks and stuffing them into the boots.

He moved closer again and pulled her belt out of the loops and unbuttoned her jeans. As soon as her zipper was down, he tugged off her jeans and stripped them away, leaving her only in her black panties. It only took a moment for him to slip those off, too. He put her panties and jeans on top of her other clothing.

He tugged at her nipple. "I want to eat you up like you ate that ice cream in Scottsdale. It was so damn hot watching you."

She swallowed, feeling suddenly shy and nervous. She started to put her arms over her breasts but he stopped her by catching her wrists in one hand.

"Oh, no you don't." He shook his head. "I want to see you."

He released her then tossed his Stetson onto her clothing before unbuttoning his western work shirt, all the while keeping his gaze fixed on her. The air felt cool on her body and her nipples were impossibly tight. She swallowed as she watched him remove his clothing, piece by piece, from his boots and socks to his belt.

Excerpt... Tying You Down

Cheyenne McCray

Butterflies traveled through Jo's belly as she and Tate headed back to her house. What was she doing, inviting him over for dinner? It was one thing to go out with him, another to have him over for dinner.

She let them into the house. It was a large home that she'd fallen in love with when she moved back to the town. She set her purse on the table in the foyer and he set his ball cap there, too, before she led him to the kitchen.

Hair had escaped her braid and she pushed it out of her face as she turned to face him. "What sounds good?"

He hitched his shoulder up against the archway into the kitchen and hooked his thumbs in the front pockets of his Wranglers. His T-shirt was pulled taut against his muscular chest and his hair was mussed from being under the ball cap. "Anything easy."

She rummaged around in the pantry and pulled out a package of angel hair pasta and a jar of three-cheese spaghetti sauce. "How about spaghetti? That's fast."

"Great." He watched her with an intense look that made her feel a little unnerved. "What can I do to help?"

"Stand there and keep looking sexy," she said without thinking.

He grinned. "Sexy, huh?"

She shrugged and tried to hide a smile. "You have your moments." She grabbed the large stockpot she used to boil water in for pasta and filled it with water.

While the water heated, she washed up then cut thick slices of the French bread she had just bought and made several pieces of garlic bread with fresh garlic and olive oil. When the water was boiling, she put the angel hair pasta in then grabbed a package of pre-made salad from the fridge and put it into a bowl.

They talked as she put together the simple dinner and he set the table with dishes she got out of the cabinet and silverware from a drawer. He also set out the wine glasses and opened a bottle of Merlot from her wine rack. She kept wine on hand even though she only drank if she had company.

She was glad he was so easy to talk with and there weren't any lulls in conversation.

When dinner was ready and on the table, they both slid into their chairs. They sat at the small table in the kitchen rather than the large one in the dining room.

She served a huge pile of spaghetti in his pasta bowl before serving herself a much smaller amount. She was hungry, but she couldn't help feeling like she was overdoing it today. She forced herself to shove aside thoughts of the chilidog, and bites of curly fries, and chocolate cake she'd had earlier. Spaghetti and a high-calorie day wasn't going to hurt her. It was something she had to remind herself all the time. Counselors had told her that her fear of eating too much was something she'd probably have to work through for the rest of her life, and she'd found that to be true.

"I had a great time today." She smiled at him after she'd eaten some of the pasta and a piece of garlic toast. "I don't know if I've had that much fun in a long time, especially on a date."

He returned her smile. "There's more where that came from."

She took a sip of her Merlot then set her glass down. "Angling for another date?"

"Is it working?" he asked as he twirled the pasta on his fork.

"Maybe." She felt a warmth inside her that she hadn't felt in a long time. A sense of contentment that probably should have scared her, but right now it didn't.

She thought about Tate's old girlfriend and wondered how much time he'd spent with her at lunch and what he and Daphne had talked about. But that wasn't any of her business and if she said anything it would make it sound like she was jealous. She wasn't, of course. She had nothing to be jealous of and no reason to be.

As they ate, she would take him in from beneath her lashes. He was so large and virile, an alpha male that drew her for so many reasons. She enjoyed being around him and the fact was she was incredibly attracted to him, both mentally and physically.

If he was everything he seemed to be, he was a good guy, too, like Charlee had said.

After they put the small amount of leftovers away and loaded the dishes in the dishwasher, they walked out of the kitchen into the living room.

He looked at her when they came to a halt. "I had a great day, Jo. Thank you for saying yes."

She slipped her hands into her back pockets to keep herself from touching him. She wanted nothing more than to feel his chest beneath her palms, his hair sliding through her fingers, his body tight against hers. And the way he was looking at her was enough to make her forget everything…forget every last hesitation she might have.

He reached up and skimmed her cheek with his fingertips, his green eyes studying her for a long moment. He cupped her face in his palms and slowly began lowering his head toward hers.

She caught her breath, a tangle of emotions whirling through her. Fear, excitement, even a little bit of shyness.

And then his lips were pressed against hers and he was kissing her, gently exploring her mouth with his.

It was perhaps the sweetest kiss she'd ever experienced. She found herself surprised that such a dominant man could be so gentle.

She slipped her hands out of her pockets and touched him like she'd been dying to. She ran her palms over his hard biceps to his broad shoulders. Slowly she eased her hands down the firm muscles of his chest before moving back to his shoulders.

Wanting more and more of him, she clenched her fingers in his T-shirt and pressed her mouth more firmly to his. She became the aggressor, desiring him so much that her entire body ached for him.

He answered her with a groan and matched the strength of her kiss until he was dominating her. She loved a man in control when it came to passion and sex and she had a feeling that Tate could be everything she wanted and more.

She moaned as he grasped her hip with one of his large hands and pulled her tight up against him as he slipped his hand into her hair and cupped the back of her head.

His erection was large and rigid against her and a thrill went through her from her belly to the place between her thighs that now ached to have him fill her. Her nipples were hard and tight as his chest pressed against her breasts.

She slid her arms to his neck, her hunger fierce, unbridled. He grasped her ass in both hands and then she wrapped her thighs around his hips and he was carrying her.

The next thing she knew, her back was up against the wall, his jean-clad cock pressed against her hot center. She wished her own jeans were gone as well as his and that he was sliding into her now.

Her mind spun from the kiss and she could barely breathe. He moved one of his hands beneath her top and his palm cupped her breast through the satin of her bra. She gasped as he fondled and pinched her nipple.

He broke the kiss and she tilted her head back as he moved his lips down the column of her throat to the V of her blouse. He shoved up the material and pulled down her bra, exposing her breasts to his gaze.

Her nipples tightened ever more and she gave a loud moan as he ran his tongue over each of the hard nubs. She slid her hands into his hair, pressing him tighter to her breasts as he sucked and licked one nipple and then the other.

He moved his hips, rubbing his cock against her, mimicking what he would do when he took her. His cock was so rigid and hard that it felt like it could bruise her if he pressed any harder.

Excerpt... Fencing You In

Cheyenne McCray

"I don't date playboys." Tess Grady wiped down the bar, shaking her head and trying not to smile as she looked at Gage McBride sitting on the stool in front of her. "Once again, the answer is no."

"Playboy?" The cowboy raised a brow as he set down his cold mug of beer. "Now I'm a playboy?"

"A cowboy with a girl in every town." Tess began polishing a glass. "I've heard the rumors."

"You believe everything you hear?" An amused smile curved the corner of his mouth. "Don't tell me you judge a man based on rumors."

She shrugged one shoulder. "If the Stetson fits…"

He leaned forward, folding his muscular arms on the bar. Hell, every part of the man appeared muscular. She was loath to admit it, but the thought of undressing such a hot package made her mouth water. "Why don't you get to know me?" he asked. "Judge for yourself."

As she polished another glass, she tried to ignore the pull the cowboy had on her. Ever since Nectars had opened, Gage had been coming into the bar and would flirt with her when she wasn't working in the Hummingbird, the restaurant side of her family's establishment. Most of the time, she was in the restaurant so she didn't see Gage often enough for him to corner her like he had now.

When he was near, he set her senses on fire, and she always tried to find a way to get away from the man as fast as possible. Unfortunately, today wasn't a day she could escape because they were short-staffed in the bar.

She blew a blonde curl out of her eyes. "No thanks," she said despite the fact that she was so very tempted.

Clear green eyes without a hint of hazel in them studied her. His eyes held the kind of sensuality that caused a woman's belly to squirm. He had dark hair and just enough stubble on his jaws to add to his rough, sexy appearance.

The tempting thing with Gage was that rough and sexy was natural. He was not some guy trying to look like a hardworking cowboy. She'd been told how successful his water well drilling business was and that he might play hard but he worked even harder. Of course, she'd never let him know she'd been intrigued enough to learn more about him. She found it curious and rather attractive that he never mentioned his business success to lure her in.

"Come on, Tess." Gage's sexy drawl was enough to make her toes curl. "One date."

She opened her mouth to respond when she saw a tall, gorgeous redhead making a beeline through the establishment, headed straight for Gage. A flare of heat was in the woman's gaze and she looked like she could spit flames.

She came up behind Gage, so angry looking that Tess could imagine the woman's eyes glowing red. "Well hello, Gage." The redhead spat the words with venom.

A pained expression crossed his face and Tess thought she might have seen him wince.

Slowly he turned toward the redhead and smiled. "Hi, Nandra."

"You—" Nandra raised her hand and slapped Gage hard across his left cheek "—*bastard.*" The sound of her hand contacting flesh was loud.

The few patrons in the bar went quiet.

The woman cut her gaze to Tess. "So you're his little squeeze now? Just don't get too comfortable." Nandra spun around and marched out of the bar, her heels clicking on the wood floor.

Gage watched Nandra walk out as he rubbed his jaw while talking resumed. Fortunately, those in the bar all had full drinks and Tess could enjoy Gage's discomfort.

He looked back at Tess as she was trying to hold back laughter. He picked up his cold beer mug and put it against the side of his face. "She packs some power."

"You have a way with the ladies." Tess looked at him with amusement.

"Second time this month." He gave a rueful smile as he lowered his mug to the bar. "I guess you might as well just slap me now and get it over with."

Tess did laugh then. "Assuming I'd be foolish enough go out with you to begin with." She gestured toward the entrance. "And that was not the best endorsement." She braced her hands on the bar. "I suppose you didn't deserve that."

"No, I deserved it." His admission surprised Tess. "Long story."

She leaned down and rested her elbow on the bar, her chin in her hand. "The bar is nearly empty. I have time."

He grinned. "Go out with me and I'll tell you whatever you want to know."

She rolled her eyes. "Good try."

"How about tomorrow night?" His green eyes held hers and she knew exactly what a romance heroine meant when she felt like she was melting. She felt like her bones had gone soft and she was breathing a little faster.

Damn.

She pushed away from the bar and felt like she had to physically break the connection with him to do so. "I'm busy."

"Is that right?" he said.

"My daughter has a kindergarten open house." Tess smiled at the thought of Jenny then felt an immediate stab of guilt that she had to work so late when she should be home with her.

Gage started to say something but to Tess's relief, a crowd of young adults pushed their way into Nectars.

"Excuse me." She gave Gage a quick smile then moved down the bar to where one of the young men had come up to order. "I'll need to see your ID," she said to the guy. He pulled out his driver's license and handed it to her. The license had the name Hal Johnson on it. When she returned it, she gave a nod in the direction of the two young women and another young man who sat as a nearby table. "Theirs, too, if they're ordering drinks, Hal."

Hal looked a little annoyed, but said "All right."

After checking everyone's ID and making sure they were at least twenty-one, Tess took their orders and served up beers for them.

When she finished with that group, two separate couples walked through the door. The evening crowd had begun to filter in. She glanced back to where Gage had been sitting and saw that he was gone, and that once again he'd left a generous tip sticking out from beneath his beer mug.

Even though he'd left, she still felt as if she could sense him watching her. Warmth spread over her skin as if he was touching her now. Just thinking about the man was going to drive her crazy. She shook her head. Damn.

There was something about Gage McBride that intrigued her in ways she couldn't begin to understand. She liked solid, dependable men like the man she'd married. Steve had died from a car accident some time ago and she hadn't dated anyone since he'd passed away. Pain still squeezed her heart when she thought about him but the pain had faded enough that maybe she should start dating again.

But *not* a sexy cowboy ladies man. That was not smart. Not smart at all.

Excerpt... Roping Your Heart

Cheyenne McCray

"I guess that will have to do for today." Cat brushed her hair out of her eyes as she started to organize the papers on Blake's desk. "We can work on this more another day." She glanced from the papers to him. He was sitting in the chair beside her now, in front of the desk. "My schedule is still pretty open," she said. "When is a good time for us to get together again?"

He was studying her, his gaze so intense that she felt the heat of it on her skin. "Friday night at seven," he said.

"Friday night?" It took a moment to register that he was asking her out. "Oh." She hesitated and he kept looking at her with that same dark look. "I—sure."

She felt warning bells going off in her head, but too late. It wasn't good to spend so much time with the man. She was going to fall head over heels for him again.

If she hadn't already.

She looked away from the intensity of his gaze and got to her feet. From her peripheral vision she saw him stand, then felt the heat of his body when he moved closer to her.

"I think we made pretty good progress." Her heart pounded faster and she busied herself with making each stack on the desktop perfectly neat. "We might be able to get everything done in one more meeting." She rushed her words, feeling like she was babbling.

"KitCat." His voice was soft and she went still at the low, throbbing quality of it.

Slowly, she lifted her eyes to meet his. He was looking at her intently. Her lips parted, but she couldn't think of a thing to say.

He took her by the shoulders, bringing her face to face with him. "Damn, Cat. I don't know how much longer I can be around you without having you."

Her eyes widened and her lips parted. He wanted her?

He gripped her upper arms tighter, the pressure of his fingers almost hurting her. "Damn," he said again before he jerked her up against him and brought his mouth hard down on hers.

She gasped as he took control of her mouth, kissing her hard. It was more primal than the night before, almost wild. She didn't remember him kissing like this before. It was as if the man he had been before had matured, becoming more dominant and decisive. She knew he'd decided he was going to have her. If she said no, he'd let her go, but she didn't want to say no. She wanted him.

A groan rose up in him and she followed his lead, letting him take the kiss to a level of passion she'd never experienced before. He released her shoulders and slid his hands over her blouse to her waist then cupped her ass and pulled her up tight to him. The feel of his erection against her belly sent fire through her straight between her thighs.

She breathed in his clean, masculine scent and reveled in his taste and the feel of his hands on her. She moved her hands up his chest, feeling the soft cotton of his T-shirt beneath her palms, and then she wrapped her arms around his neck and pressed her breasts against him.

When he broke the kiss, he moved his lips along her jawline to her throat. His stubble felt rough against her skin but something about the sandpapery feel of it made her even more excited.

"I'm not going to be able to help myself with you." He groaned as he pulled her short skirt above her ass and felt the silky panties underneath. The heat of his palms burned through the thin material to her skin and it almost felt like she was wearing nothing at all. "Hell, you'd better tell me now if you want to stop."

"Don't stop." She moaned, as he trailed his lips and tongue from the hollow of her throat to the V in her blouse.

He whirled her so that she was backed up against the desk and she had to brace her hands on the stacks of papers to either side of her in order to balance herself. She arched her back as he moved his hands to the buttons on her blouse. His big fingers fumbled with the buttons and he gave a low growl and grasped the material.

Buttons flew and she gasped as he tore the blouse open. She heard the ping of buttons but was barely conscious of them as he pushed her blouse over her shoulders and down her arms before she shook it the rest of the way off.

About Cheyenne

New York Times and *USA Today* bestselling author Cheyenne McCray's books have received multiple awards and nominations, including

RT Book Reviews magazine's Reviewer's Choice awards for Best Erotic Romance of the year and Best Paranormal Action Adventure of the year

*Three "RT Book Reviews" nominations, including Best Erotic Romance, Best Romantic Suspense, and Best Paranormal Action Adventure.

*Golden Quill award for Best Erotic Romance

*The Road to Romance's Reviewer's Choice Award

*Gold Star Award from Just Erotic Romance Reviews

*CAPA award from The Romance Studio

Cheyenne grew up on a ranch in southeastern Arizona. She has been writing ever since she can remember, back to her kindergarten days when she penned her first poem. She always knew one day she would write novels, hoping her readers would get lost in the worlds she created, just as she experienced when she read some of her favorite books.

Chey has three sons, two dogs, and is an Arizona native who loves the desert, the sunshine, and the beautiful sunsets. Visit Chey's website and get all of the latest info at her website (http://www.cheyennemccray.com) and meet up with her at Cheyenne McCray's Place on Facebook (https://www.facebook.com/CheyenneMcCraysPlace)!

CPSIA information can be obtained at www.ICGtesting.com
Printed in the USA
LVOW12s1546121113

361027LV00016B/597/P